LOVE *Me*

LOVE ENDURES • BOOK TWO

SUSAN WARNER

Published by EG Publishing, 2019
First Edition. December 22, 2019

LOVE *Me*

One

Gina Kenyon had come a long way to find a thief. Christopher Griggs might be a CEO, but if the thief shoe fit, she was sure going to make him wear it. There weren't words for his blatant boldness of hoodwinkery. She didn't even know if that was a word, but it didn't matter. What mattered was this morning,

Gina had walked into Cora Thalman's office, her boss at Vision Consulting, and was handed a project. That, in and of itself, wasn't an issue. She was one of the best project managers in the company. It wasn't an issue when Cora told her that Vision needed to get this account. Mr. Griggs had already sent back three project managers. The problem was it was her project. She had put in her hard work and time to create it. Gina's project plans were distinctive in the detail and efficiency, so much so she didn't understand how anyone thought they could steal one.

Mr. Griggs had a lot to answer for. It was bad enough there was only one place he could have gotten the project from—but she didn't want to think about that because that was a mistake she was desperately trying to forget.

Griggs owned Chymera Corporations. It was known for eating up little companies and adding it to their conglomerate or dismantling companies that were in its way. Chymera worked in the tech industries and government contracts.

Gina tried to remember the calming conversation she had practiced with her friend, Natalie. Natalie was always trying to help her with ways to keep calm. She needed to practice being calm before she met the thief who was trying to abscond with her work.

Gina tried to give him the benefit of the doubt as she walked through the front doors of the New Hope Center. Maybe Griggs wasn't the thieving person she thought he was.

When she stepped into the foyer, the first thing she noticed was an older woman sitting at a desk with what looked like large butterflies in her hair. Gina could see the coiled springs that kept the wings attached and moving with every movement of the woman's head and every breeze that went through the foyer.

"Can I help you?" the older woman asked. Gina pulled her gaze away from the bright butterflies and tried to find the words to respond. Now that she was up close it was clear that the butterflies were perched in auburn hair that was definitely attached to a wig. Gina could tell as it was just a smidgen off-Center, leaving a little bit of the woman's natural hair exposed.

Gina supposed she was taking too long to answer, and then the woman reached up and touched the exposed spot and then laughed.

"Don't worry, I know it's peeking out. It was itching this morning, and I gave up. Decided that I'm old enough to do what I want, and my comfort was way more important than the look. What can I do for you?"

Gina walked closer to the desk, pulled in by the woman's smile.

"I'm here to see Mr. Griggs," Gina said with a smile of her own.

The woman transformed right before her. Where there had been a smiling woman who was undoubtedly someone's grandmother, sat an angry woman with pursed lips and little patience. She crossed her arms in front of her chest and gave Gina a narrowed gazed.

"You? With him?" she asked incredulously.

"He asked me to meet him here," Gina replied.

"My name is Daisy. You look like a nice girl," Daisy said as if seeing Griggs and being a nice girl was a total contradiction.

A door opened on the left, and out came a small man, about five foot two with grey hair. He had a thin frame and an easy smile.

He walked behind the desk, and Daisy looked at him.

"Tim, she's here to see Griggs."

Tim looked Gina over from head to toe and shook his head before speaking.

"I guess you can't tell anymore. She looks like such a nice girl," he murmured.

Gina was about to comment when she saw Daisy reach over to her phone and then call out. "Griggs, come out here!"

Gina didn't have time to be shocked because the same door that Tim had come through slammed open and a tall, handsome man stepped into the foyer.

"You!" exclaimed Gina.

The man looked up to see Gina and sucked his teeth. "This day just isn't going to get any be better."

"Well, I guess you shouldn't expect good things when you steal," Gina spat back. She turned back to Daisy. "Call Mr. Griggs; he'll want to know about this man."

Daisy and Tim looked confused and didn't move. Gina got ready to explain when he spoke.

"Gina, my full name is Christopher Alex Myers Griggs. Myers is my mother's maiden name."

Gina turned back to Christopher and tried to comprehend what was going on.

"You're Griggs, and you're Myers?" This day was just spiraling out of control. Gina had been primed to tell the CEO, Mr. Griggs that he had some gall to request her to implement the plan he stole from her company. Now that she had met Mr. Griggs it was all clear.

The man before her she knew as Alex Myers, the nice man she attended the project management classes with for the last year and a half. Then he just disappeared. No notice, no warning just got up and left. She had thought she and Alex were getting close but when he just disappeared she tried to toss it up as one of those things.

Now she knew how Mr. Griggs had gotten her project. This project was the one they had both worked on in class together. He hadn't just disappeared. He had stolen their project and now here he was.

"Yes, if you will come with me, I'll explain—" Christopher said as he was cut off by Daisy.

"I bet he will," Daisy said with a snort.

"Don't fall for his foolishness, girl. You seem really nice," Tim chimed in.

Gina knew her face was set in grim resolution as she walked through the door. She followed him down the hall and tried to focus. It didn't matter what his name was. She knew what he was. He was six feet of well-muscled predator. The charcoal gray suit he wore couldn't hide that raw, animal aura that surrounded him. It wasn't just his jet black hair and hypnotic sable brown eyes, it was the man himself that first attracted her to him a year ago before he broke her heart.

They walked down the hall into an office, and when she stepped in, she turned and eyed him cautiously as he closed the door. She could feel her heart beating faster and her breath coming in short rasps. What was wrong with her? This man—no matter what his name—was a trickster, a fake, a thief, and an opportunist. However, even knowing what she knew, he still had the power to make her uneasy. It didn't help that she was five feet, eight inches. It meant that on top of everything else, he could loom over her.

"So whoever you are, I'm sure you can come up with a good story for all of this," Gina stated. Gina didn't have a family, she was a product of multiple foster homes. None of them were bad, they just weren't family, and they weren't hers. Sometimes she thought this was why she didn't play well with others.

"I told you who I am," Christopher said. "I need you to listen to me, so I can explain."

"Explain? Why should I listen? What new story will you spin now?" Gina balled her hands into fists to stop herself from giving in to the silky tones that seemed to wrap themselves around her self resolve. What was wrong with her? She knew he couldn't be trusted. No man had ever had this effect on her. Of all people why did it have to be him she had to deal with now?

"I made a mistake. Okay, I made a bunch of mistakes," Christopher murmured softly.

"Mistakes? Not very original for a CEO. Listen, the past is the past. Why am I here?"

"I've been trying to find the best way to contact you and explain. In the end, I thought this would be the best way. I also need your help."

"You lie to me, steal my work, and now you need my help?" she asked incredulously.

"Hear me out," he said with his hands up.

Her brain was saying walk out the door and go home. Unfortunately, it seemed that organ wasn't in control. Gina had to admit Christopher was easy on the eyes and could talk a smooth game. It was his eyes. When he fixed them on her, she could feel a coil of excitement unfurl in her. She wanted to look away, but she wouldn't give him the satisfaction of knowing he unnerved her in any way. She felt like Little Red Riding Hood, and the wolf was inviting her to dinner at his place to talk.

"Everyone gets a free consultation hour. If you want to waste yours trying to explain, go right ahead," Gina said, tucking a strand of hair behind her ear.

"You know I own Chymera corp."

"I know now," Gina muttered.

"Well, I do, and we acquire, dismantle, or absorb companies. It's old, and I wanted to do something new. I bought this Health Center about a year and a half ago."

Gina looked around the office they were in. The walls were grey with time and a dusting of dirt. The floor was old linoleum just like the front, and the furniture looked as though it had been salvaged from what the garage sales wouldn't take. Two fold-up chairs against the wall. A wooden desk that, if she wasn't mistaken, had a tilt to it as if one of the legs was a bit short.

"Well, you haven't left much of a mark around here. No one would mistake this for one of your businesses in the city."

Christopher sat down in the chair and for a moment, Gina held her breath, unsure if the chair was strong enough to hold him, if it wasn't she would find herself having to pick him up from the floor.

"That was the point. I used all of the techniques I had always used, and nothing I did here seemed to help. My COO is my sister Gwen. She looked at this place and said it was a waste and that I was wasting my money."

"So, this place is a dare for you?"

Christopher sighed. "It might have been when I bought it, but I've been here with them for the last year, and they've grown on me. It's true its an acquired taste. Even Daisy at the front has grown on me, but I have to tell you, Healthcare isn't the same as business, and the things I know don't translate the way I wanted. So I went back to school. I took a course using my middle and mother's maiden name. I made sure it was at night, and then I met you."

"For a year, Alex! Or Chris, or whatever! You couldn't tell me during the year we dated?" Gina asked.

"The truth of it was I thought things would change if you knew I had money."

"Did I seem that shallow?"

"NO!"

"Maybe I seemed like a money-grubber?"

"No, Gina never."

"Then maybe—"

"It wasn't you. It was me."

"Oh, we've all heard that one before Chris—"

"I enjoyed being with you," Chris said softly. "Gina, you're bold, direct, and beautiful. You make no apologies for your thoughts, and you always say it straight and—"

"After two semesters and us doing a project, which just so happens to be in healthcare, you disappeared and then stole my project!"

Chris stood up and held his arms wide. "When you say it like that, it sounds bad. It didn't happen like that for me, but I can see—"

"Can you see why I'm thinking the smart thing to do is to walk out the door, Chris? Can you see that?" she said with her hand on her hip and her shoe tapping away.

Chris stopped and looked at her. "I can see we are about to negotiate."

Gina stood under his gaze for a moment and tried hard not to fidget and to hold on to her anger. Why was he watching her like that? She wanted to touch her hair and smooth her clothing. What was he looking at so intently? Then when she saw the light, male interest in his eye, she stood a little taller and squared her shoulders. She wasn't his height, but she wouldn't slump or hide. She walked boldly to his chair and looked down at him.

"You don't have anything I want."

Chris stood up and moved the chair aside. It took all of two seconds for him to turn the tables on her. "I'm sorry, Gina. I was wrong. Let's start over."

When did his lips become so intriguing? She closed her eyes and took a breath.

"You're wasting your time," she said through clenched teeth.

"What if I told you I wanted you to reconsider staying for the Center's sake and not mine?"

Gina looked at him sideways and remembered an article she had read about him. In it, they called him The Closer. He was living up to that title today. He was a hawk, watching every movement she made.

Being this close to him gave her a better view of him as well. Chris was impressive in the distance, but up close and personal, he was a force of nature. She could feel power radiating off of him and sending shivers down her spine.

"Don't you think that's a bit of a reach even for you?" This close, he was making her nervous. She was confused by the conflicting signs and feelings that she was trying to manage while presenting a cool façade to Chris.

"What I think is I screwed up. I might have thought what I did was for the right reasons, but I was wrong. Give me a month. Get to know me and let me show you who I really am. I'm asking for a chance, and while we're here, we can help this Center."

Gina played the offer around in her head. It was a plan she knew. This was an account she knew her boss said she had to get, and it was in a field she excelled in.

"Just out of curiosity, how would you explain me to everyone?"

Chris' smile widened. "I'll take care of that. Do we have a deal?"

Make a deal with Christopher. What was she thinking? Better yet, what she didn't need to be thinking about was how sexy his voice was. Gina could feel sparks racing along her body as his smooth voice undulated through her. Of all the men to finally have a reaction to, it had to be him!

Not one to back down from a fight or leave others in need, Gina already knew her answer. She looked up at him and glowered.

"I'll stay for the Center, and when I'm done, I'm done. Nothing more between you and me. You lied to me and I don't think I can trust you. Take it or leave it."

Chris smiled and nodded. "I'll take…you—I mean, I accept your deal."

"Dream on Mr. CEO. I'm here for the Center. I'll call to contact you in a couple of days to start." She didn't wait for a response. Instead, she stepped away and walked out of the Center. When she got back to her car, she looked at the Center and sighed.

"Gina girl, what have you done?"

Two

Chris stood in the room and listened to her walk down the hall and out the door. He had to stop himself from running after her. They both needed time to regroup.

The office door opened slowly, and he didn't need to look behind him to see who it was. The breeze from the hallway wafted in the aroma of baby powder. He didn't know how Daisy did it, but she was a walking advertisement for Johnson and Johnson.

"What is the possibility that you are going to go back to the front desk?"

"Slim and non-existent," Daisy said to Chris.

"Then say it and be done with it."

"You know I'm not one to be in your business—"

Chris turned and looked at Daisy, who stood at the door looking at him as if she didn't know why he was surprised by that statement.

"Why are you looking at me like that?" she asked.

Chris turned and waved her on.

"No, go ahead. It's just the way my day is going to end," droned Chris.

"Well, like I was saying. I try not to get into your business, but she seemed like a nice girl. She came in alone, and I want to make sure she was okay and all."

Chris looked at Daisy, and she had gone from inching into the room to a warrior woman standing firm, waiting for his answer.

"Her name Gina Keynon, and if all works out, she'll be our guardian angel," Chris said.

"She seemed like a very nice girl. Definitely not the type I expect to see around you. You know a nice girl.," Daisy said doubtfully.

Chris thought back to Gina and him staying up late many nights, arguing over her project plan. Chris knew that the sultry tones of her voice deflected people from the sheer determination of will that was housed in her petite frame. Gina was stubborn, and she didn't look at the size of the mountain or the difficulty of the task before her, she just went forward. It was her spirit that drew him, the other attributes like her wit, playfulness, and loyalty were extras he never expected to find.

"Gina isn't as defenseless as you might think," Chris replied.

"That nice little girl? I know a good girl when I see it, and I'm telling you that no matter what happens to us here, you should do right by her."

"Why do you think you need to defend Gina?"

"She may be a capable young woman, but we're talking about you. How can a young woman defend herself from someone like you?" Daisy said skeptically.

Chris thought about the time he had spent with her and the reason he had disappeared out of her life. This was one point that he and Daisy could agree on, and those were far and few in between.

Being together with Gina in school was one thing, but he had to go back to the corporate world and his Gina wasn't the kind of woman to survive in it. She was too kind, passionate and considerate. She thought about the greater good when everyone else was thinking about money. In fact, what made her project plan so great was the fact that she took the people into consideration. She put herself in their place and created plans that everyone could buy into. Everyone couldn't implement it but then that was why she was the one who needed to implement it.

Chris thought about their meeting today and recalled the way her clothes moved with her body, giving hints to the curves below. She didn't accentuate her looks but let her work speak for itself. It made her twice as attractive to him when she bowled him over with numbers and stats on why her plans would work. He hadn't realized it until today but he hadn't felt this sense of anticipation in a while. This community health project was important to him and with Gina here, it felt like his first and most important deal of his life.

"You do know I can wait here all day for you to answer me?" Daisy threatened.

"I'm not the devil you'd paint me to be," Chris said as he turned to face Daisy.

"Okay come with me."

With his curiosity peaked, Chris rose and followed Daisy. She walked out of the office and went down the hall, out the door and to the lobby. Tim looked up to see the both of them walking out the door. Chris had to admit he was just as confused as Tim. They walked out of the front door until they were on the sidewalk.

Daisy turned to him and spread her arms wide. "What do you see?"

Chris looked around. The building was on the corner of a service road and a highway. The property was bordered by an empty lot that had turned into a mini swampland. To the left of the building there was a small park for people with kids to wait.

He turned back to Daisy. "I see a Center in the middle of nowhere that is the last hold out for people in need."

Daisy cocked her head to the side and smirked. "The last two people who came here and tried to buy the Center saw a building next to a plot of land that was worth millions if the Center went away. We were just a bump in the road to them making another mall. Then you buy it. The man who was known to make things go away and convert to bigger things. How did you expect us to see you?"

Chris nodded and shrugged. "I expected a shot. Just like you give the people who walk in your doors every day. I expected a shot to be judged on what I did not what I looked like."

Chris looked at Daisy and took a breath. He respected the strength and courage it took for her to bring him out here and speak. She hadn't given him a long speech or brought pictures, it was just the facts. It wasn't the first time she'd spoken to him plainly, she was consistent in that all the time.

"You were judged on what you did Mr. CEO of Chymera."

Chris held up his hands. "I'm working on it Daisy. Gina will make this all work."

Daisy grumbled. "So you're using her?"

Chris sighed and shook his head. "No, I'm hoping she'll get to know me again in the process and keep me when she's done."

Daisy looked at him skeptically. "You saying you have feelings for that young lady?"

Chris smiled. "You ask more questions than my sister."

"Stop avoiding the question," Daisy persisted.

"I've got feelings for her," he murmured. Daisy started laughing. She laughed so much she bent over and slapped her knee.

"Well, if you had told me that earlier I'd have known that we don't have anything to worry about. You won't be selling this place any time soon."

Chris was confused. "I don't get it."

Daisy walked up to him and patted him on the shoulder as she went to the front door.

"I've never known a man to be able to concentrate fully on two things. If you're trying to get this woman, then I don't need to worry about you selling it off for now. It gives us time, and me some entertainment, because the woman who left here today did not seem like she knew any of your finer qualities."

Three

Chris knew this day would come but it surprised him how quickly it arrived. He had shown up at the Center this morning and Daisy told him his sister Julia was waiting in the large classroom in the back. This classroom was called the garden room as it had a set of doors that led out to the back of the building where a small garden was growning.

When he walked into the room he saw Julia looking out the double doors to the backyard. She looked like a beautiful painting, standing at the door with the rays of sunshine obscuring her features but outlining her pose.

Chris loved his sister and under normal circumstances he would be glad to see her but since he had bought this Center, the relationship between them had been strained.

"You spoke to Gina yesterday and to date I have no contract from the consulting firm or any indication that she will accept," Julia Griggs said. "It was a valiant try but I don't know why you expected a different outcome. Everything can't be washed away or forgiven for a cause. I would have thought you learned that from our father."

Julia walked away from the door and stepped out of the light. She was a copy of their mother. Julia was elegant with her auburn hair swept up in a chignon. She was a striking woman in her early fifties. Her brown eyes missed nothing when she was negotiating and today was no different. With a patrician nose she inherited from their father and a svelte figure from their mother, she was an attractive woman to all who saw her. Today she had donned a black suit and a black silk blouse. From her ears hung pearl drops, and a simple gold chain with a cross hung about her neck.

They never argued over business but this Center had proven to be the exception. One of the main services of the clinic was to help those who were addicted to drugs or alcohol. The problem hit too close for Julia. Their father had been an alcoholic, who had eventually gotten clean and recovered but the early days were hard and Julia never forgot or forgave.

"I don't think it's over yet. Our past got in the way of the goal but I still think Gina will give it some thought. We left with a standing deal, so we will see."

Julia gave him a wan smile. "You don't need to do this Chris. You don't owe him anything."

Chris thought of his parents. Both of them had passed. His father had died of a liver disease and his mother had faded and followed him a year later. He remembered his dad laughing up until the day he passed. Riley Griggs had a GED and a gift to be ablet to sell anything. He had been doing door to door sales when he met his wife. She had given him the confidence to be more than a door to door salesman. They had opened up an acquisitions company and quickly prospered by being able to find companies flip them and sell them.

The money had come fast and with it Riley had fallen in with a drinking crowd that didn't encourage family or a wife. Julia had been six years old around then and times were dark, as fights and drinking episodes polluted the family for almost five years. On threat of his wife leaving, Riley went into rehab and got clean.

"I don't owe him but I'd like to do something that lasts beyond me, Julia."

"Pick a charity and give them money but this…this clinic? Leave it for someone else to be their crusader."

"He rehabbed Julia," he said. "He and mom found a way together."

"Mom was an angel. There was no excuse for what he did."

Chris sighed. "I know you don't agree but can you support me in this? Until it plays out, however that is?"

"We make decisions about Chymera all the time. We do it together Chris. Does my opinion not matter in this at all?" she murmured. She walked closer to him and laid a hand on his shoulder. "Is this Center so important to you that you would ignore me? Is that the fate of Griggs women? To be ignored and have to follow a man no matter where he goes, until they come to the light, little brother?"

Chris covered her hand. "We're a team, don't make this a wedge between us."

Julia pulled her hand back and looked around the room. "Well, I guess it's all moot unless she agrees to help you. I waited for the contract yesterday when you said she had agreed but—"

"Well, she had conditions," Chris admitted. "I know she'll do it but this will be the only way she'll do it."

Julia's eyebrow rose and she paused for a moment. "Well I admit I was wrong then. A Grigg's male is not running this ship," she murmured. "I'm curious how you got her to come? I would think after all you told me she wouldn't meet you at all."

"I sent her plan to the agency she works for and rejected all of the other project managers until they sent her."

Julia laughed. "Well that is one way to go about it."

Chris gritted his teeth. "Go ahead and laugh. I just didn't have a better way."

Julia smiled. "Don't be so hard on yourself. I'm sure this is the first time you've run into the issue of someone not wanting to be around you or talk to you. So I'm really curious now. What is the next course of action if she says she refuses to help you? The directors at this site want to know so they can plan."

"I guess this is a way of bringing up their plan of I have them a quarter of a million dollars and they try to fix what's wrong here. You can just put that thought from your mind. That is not even an option. Looking at the way things are now."

Julia shook her head and implored him. "You've admitted yourself you don't have the expertise or intuition to run this Center."

Chris looked at his sister and knew that Julia could turn this Center around. She was compassionate and he couldn't think of a person who he'd trust more, but they both knew she would never take this assignment.

"If I need to I'll think about the staff here and see who can be trained, if at all."

"Chris give them a chance. We gave a little extra leeway to the directors in their departments, and you have to admit the business has picked up."

"All of them seem to like their section but I haven't seen the plan or the talent it takes to run the whole Center."

"Well you have to pick because there will be no more options," Julia said exasperated.

"Gina will come through."

"There is a significant amount of money to do this job. She hasn't even opened the email to see the numbers. It's possible she doesn't want it," Julia said gently.

Chris took a deep breath. "Let me think Julia. Until I have all the data I don't want to decide anything."

Julia walked to a nearby table along the wall of the room and picked up her clutch purse. "When you figure it out let me know."

Chris hugged his sister and let her walk out of the room. The truth of it was he didn't have an answer and he wasn't willing to think of a plan B. It was Gina or nothing. A knock on the classroom door made Chris dread turning around to see what was next.

Four

"Hey boss, you okay?"

Chris turned around to find Tim Peters standing in the doorway. Tim was an older guy who took shifts with Daisy manning the front door. Tim was one of the few men in the Center and they had quickly become friends.

"Hey Tim, I'm glad it's you. I'm always relieved to see at least one happy face."

"I've got a lot of messages from Miss Clara. She says she needs to discuss program business that won't hold long."

Chris groaned. "I'm afraid everything from Clara is an emergency. I know she's been under a lot of pressure losing staff members to help her out."

Tim nodded. "She's a bit more high strung than normal. I also got a call from Miss Robin. She told me to say it was an emergency."

"Thanks Tim for keeping me up to date."

Tim stood up a little straighter and nodded at Chris. "Mr. Chris I saw the young lady come in here. Was she the one who was going to fix everything?"

"Yes, but she didn't accept right away. She hasn't said no, but she hasn't said yes the way I'd like her to either."

Tim smiled and nodded his head. "In other words you don't know, huh?"

"I don't know," Chris mumbled.

Tim grinned. "Don't bother too much over it, you aren't the first man to strike out with a woman."

"Ouch! I didn't say I struck out. I'm saying that the first meet was a warm-up."

"Well, I don't know what happened I wasn't here but I do know you need her to get this done."

"Tim, we all need her."

"Well if she decides not to, just give me two weeks so I can call a few people and make sure I got someplace to go," Tim said solemnly. "Unless you're going to let the directors run the place."

"I'm working on it."

Tim rubbed his chin and cleared his throat. "I've been meaning to ask. Why don't you just sell this place like anyone else in your position would?"

"I can't do it."

"I think what you're doing is a great thing, but in the end I don't see the path changing unless something pulls through."

Tim was the *everything man*. He delivered goods throughout the building, picked up supplies if they ran short and stayed for technical and phone line problems. When Chris arrived he found that everyone knew Tim. Between Tim's knowledge and Chris' investment, they had held it together.

"I hear you Tim, but it's not time yet."

"And you think you should do all this for this place?"

"I think I owe it to everyone to do my best."

Tim nodded. "You are a rare breed and an unexpected surprise Mr. Griggs."

The crackling of the overhead speaker interrupted what Chris was going to say. Then Daisy's voice rang out.

"Griggs, Gina to see you."

She was certifiably crazy. As she walked down the hall she could feel the unwanted heat building in her body. When she approached the door that Daisy, the front desk woman, had directed her to, it opened and there he was. Everything in her body seized at that moment. Should she turn around and go back? Then he extended his hand out and that was the moment it was all coming down to. Would she do this again? It had all sounded so easy when she was thinking about it at home. She had decided she was going to come here on her own terms. She would retain control and she'd be the one to walk away when she decided. She wouldn't let the Center fall because of her prior issues with Chris. Her work ethic wouldn't let her do that.

Chris was at the door and he had never looked more tempting. In the doorway Gina could see the rays of the sun behind him as if he were an angel. Today the angel was dressed all in black from head to toe. His hair looked finger-combed and his shirt was dark black with a pair of matching dark jeans that looked as though they were made to fit him.

His gaze had never left her face and she could feel the sensual thrill of his focus on her. She didn't want him to know how much he affected her but his intensity was hard to ignore.

"Gina?" Chris had his hand out and he looked as though she held all the answers for him. "Are you coming in?"

Her common sense said she should run, but her body was moving of its own accord into the room. She just had to keep saying her mantra to herself.

I am in control. This is what I want. Nothing will happen unless I want it to.

Then she did what she always did when things seemed overwhelming. She pasted on a polite smile, nodded at him, and then settled into business mode.

"Of course Mr. Griggs."

She heard the door close behind her and she walked into the middle of the room and turned to face him.

"Mr. Griggs?" he asked.

"Let's just say I think at this time we need to keep it professional. I haven't made a final decision as of yet and there are some terms that we need to talk over."

Chris' eyebrow rose and a faint smile lifted the right side of his mouth. "Terms? I would have never expected you to come up with those when the fate of people are at stake."

Gina shifted her weight from left to right and then folded her arms over her chest. She was glad she had worn her shoulder bag today. She felt like she needed her hands free to deal with Chris.

"This isn't a matter of asking for something above and beyond but I think we both have to acknowledge that our meeting, and our prior history, makes this a more complicated issue than what would normally be expected."

"Agreed. So let's hear your terms."

"I have given it some thought and I think we should have an intermediary."

"What?"

"An intermediary. I know you know what that is as your company has served as one on several occasions."

"Why would I do that Gina?" Chris asked softly as he leaned against the door. She was a bit unsettled that he was taking it so well.

"I think that once people realize we previously have known each other that it would be complicated and inappropriate for me to be running things."

Chris smiled. "Ahh, you mean that you don't want people to think that you got this position by any other means…"

"That's right. After this is over I will go on with my life and I don't want my reputation to be marred by the fact that there was anything questionable in my behavior or career."

Chris closed his eyes and then let out a sigh. "I think you're right. I didn't think about what the gossips would say. You're also right that eventually someone would unearth the connection between us. However, the intermediary idea won't work for me."

Gina was stumped. She had expected resistance but she hadn't expected him to refuse outright.

Chris shrugged. "I do hear you, and I have a counteroffer."

Counteroffer? Gina had a feeling this was not going to go the way she envisioned it. Chris looked so relaxed and calm. Now she could feel a ball of nervousness building in her stomach.

"I'm listening. What is it that you suggest?"

"I think hiring you now would be a conflict of interest, but no one would say a thing if you were my fiancée."

Gina knew she looked horrified, and then when he didn't say it was a joke the realization that he was serious dawned on her. Gina opened her mouth but nothing came out. "You're serious?

"Yes."

Gina turned and looked until she found a chair to fall into. When she had dropped into the nearest chair her gaze swung up to Chris. "You do realize how crazy that sounds, right?

"I'm aware that it's out-of-the-box thinking," Chris said.

"No one will believe it," Gina said still dazed by the proposal.

"Why not? I'm sure that anyone who looks at you will understand why I'm attracted to you. You're beautiful, smart and independent. No one will question my taste. If anything they will only ask what took me so long to make a move."

Gina shook her head. "You don't know me," she protested.

"I think that's what engagements are for. You go on a couple of dates and if you both think it's working out well you put a more permanent title on it, and then you see if you can run the gauntlet through that."

Gina got up and paced in front of him. She faced him with her hands on her hips. "I don't know you either."

Chris smiled dangerously. "I'm open to fixing that at your own pace."

Gina took a step back in shock. "Chris what do you think is going to happen here?"

Chris shrugged. "I think I'm going to get the help I need in order to help the people here. While I'm doing that if we happen to realize that there might be something for us then it's a double win."

Gina shook her head. "Chris this is a dangerous game. I want to make sure the people here won't suffer when nothing happens between us."

"You're right, you don't know me. If you did you'd know that wasn't even a possibility."

Gina eyed him warily. "But I don't, so I'm sorry if I offended you."

"I think we've gone over the options. If you need time to—"

"I don't need the time. I know what my decision is," she said coolly. "I'll do it, but we have to be clear; the Center comes first in all things."

Chris smiled. "Of course. I have one other condition."

Gina raised her brow. "There's more?"

"I need us to define when the project is done."

"Ahh, well the project is done when I'm done implementing it."

Chris grinned. "Fine."

Gina wasn't sure how but she was certain that she had just been herded into an agreement where she was going to wind up on the losing end.

Five

The next morning Gina walked into the same large classroom. She thought it odd that the room wasn't being used because she heard people in all of the other rooms. When she went to the door she opened it without thinking. Chris and the man Daisy had introduced as Tim, were talking to one another.

Tim saw her first and his eyes widened for a moment, and then Gina thought she saw a flash of hostility cross his face but it was gone as quick as it had come. Chris turned to see her and smiled. "I'm going to visit a sister site that does what we do here. You can meet everyone here while I'm gone or you can wait. I'll be gone starting from late afternoon until tomorrow. If you have any questions ask Tim, he knows everything."

Gina nodded. "No problem. He comes highly recommended by Daisy."

"Great, I'm sure the two of you will get along just fine. I've already explained to Tim that you've agreed to help me out. Having a fiancée in the business is a great help to me now."

Tim nodded and then left the room. Gina waited until the door was closed and then she turned to face Chris.

He held up his hands in front of him. "Whoa. I don't know a lot but I know that when a woman gets that look on her face it doesn't bode well for any man around."

"We didn't talk about when you were going to tell the others or how. I wish you would think to include me before you tell everyone so we will be on the same page."

"I didn't want you to be stressed over a small detail when the whole project of fixing the Center was ahead of us."

Gina took a double take and tried to say something but the words wouldn't come out right away. "A small issue?"

"Okay not a small issue but one I tried to help out with," he said.

"If you had been spending as much time looking at the books of this Center as you were looking at how to handle the small details you might have been able to run it better."

"Hey I've been trying to get the best help to make it better."

"Yes, well I looked at the files you sent over with the proposal and I can tell you it is a mess on several levels."

Chris tightened his jaw and nodded. "You're right. I've been trying to do it all but this isn't my arena."

"Yeah, I saw that last night as I reviewed the records."

Chris stopped and looked at her. "What did you find?"

"Well, what I can say is that some of the issues seem to stem from poor processes. The directors seem to know the clinical side but money is just flowing through here."

Chris was statue still. "Money flowing through here is never a phrase an owner or investor wants to hear." Chris walked around the room and ran his hands through his hair. "Well that certainly puts a wrinkle in things. This is going to be our own guess as to who's the bad guy."

Gina tsked and looked at him intently across the room. "I hate to say it but I don't think this should be that big of a shock to you. I mean you are the CEO of Chymera. I imagine people are always trying to smuggle, steal or somehow get one over on you."

"It's true but this is s a small project. If someone is doing something like that then it's probably someone I've seen and spoken to. It's a little different when the person who's stealing from you is a person you know."

Gina watched Chris thinking it over and cleared her throat, trying to bring his attention back to the present and not to the fact that betrayal was near. Betrayal hurt no matter who you were.

"Hey, do you have time for lunch before you go? I know it's early but you need to eat right?"

How did she get into these situations? Why did she invite him out to lunch? Gina had scouted the area earlier. When he said yes she stood there in shock, but she recovered as quickly as she could and gave him the address. She was already weak and her head wasn't in control as much as she wanted it to be, she wasn't going to push fate by putting the both of them in the same car. She gave him the address and then said she'd meet him there.

Gina had found a nearby spot called The Tower. It was a mom-and-pop spot but they made a good burger. They also gave you food without being judgemental on the amount you ate. She had gone to another diner and ordered an appetizer and a burger. Then the waitress had asked when her party was going to arrive. After a hostile silence Gina ate her meal but decided in the future to find a place where she could eat unrestrained. The Tower fit the bill.

After coming for two days she befriened one of the younger waitresses, Lucy. Lucy was 19 and a single mom. She still lived at home and was chaty but harmless. Gina knew when she showed up there would be questions about Chris. When she walked into the diner, she could see that Chris had made it before her. She wasn't surprised. To be honest, Gina had taken the long way, trying to compose herself before she had to face him again.

Chris stood when he spotted her. When he stood, he looked like a lion stretching his lean body. It didn't matter what he wore. Chris was the kind of man that made his clothes look good. When he moved, his shirts moved with him and hinted at the muscle beneath it.

What didn't this man have? she thought as she moved closer.

Now she worried about her appearance. Maybe she should have put on her heels instead of the flats? She wasn't tall, but she had great legs. She had business dresses as well she could wear. These thoughts just confirmed she was still torn about wanting to please this man and wanting to finish this job and put Chris behind her. He sent her thoughts into such a tizzy she often wondered if she needed to make a project plan to manage their interactions. Today it was her kindness that had led her here. She just needed to remember that Chris was being betrayed, and not even Chris deserved that.

Gina spotted Lucy, who was staring at Chris with wide eyes and obvious interest. Gina knew if she kept her mouth open any longer, she'd get dry mouth or something would fly in it. Gina cleared her throat and Lucy blinked, turned towards Gina, and smiled as she came over.

"Are you with him?" she asked raising an eyebrow. Her blonde hair was in a French braid tied off with a neon pink scrunchie. As Lucy was talking, Chris was coming towards them. Lucy was focused on her, but in no time, Chris was behind Lucy.

"I'm with her, if she'll have me," Chris said, then held out his hand for Gina to take it.

Once again, Chris had done the unexpected. Without a thought she put her hand in his, and suddenly became very aware of the texture of his hands. They were smooth but still had calluses here and there. When his hand closed over hers, she felt like she had just fallen down the rabbit hole, and he was there to catch her. This was what his touch was doing, and he wasn't even trying. It was almost like they were back in classes with each other. That same close feelings that never had to be explained. It just confirmed in Gina's head that she was in trouble.

They walked to the booth and took seats across from each other. Lucy came to the table and stood behind Gina.

"This one isn't bad at all," she said, leaning over and whispering in her ear. Gina didn't know why she even bothered. Gina could tell from Chris' smile that he had heard the words too.

"I'm new to the area, and Gina told me to come here," Chris said.

"Wow, and you're new to the area?" Lucy stood up and nudged Gina on the shoulder. "Girl, you move quick. Good going."

"Lucy, lunch?"

Lucy came out of her fog and brought out her pad. "Oh yeah, sorry, what will you have?"

Chris put down his menu and looked at Gina. "I'll take whatever she's having," Chris said with a smile.

Lucy looked at Gina and put her notepad away before speaking. "The regular?"

Gina nodded. When Lucy left, Gina asked. "Don't you want to know what you ordered?"

He shrugged. "It doesn't matter. I'm not a picky eater, and no matter what comes out, it was so worth it to hear her say you picked me up before the rest of them."

"Sorry," Gina said as she shook her head and thought about the talk she would have with Lucy later. "I'd forgotten how young Lucy was. She's still moved by a pretty face."

"Is that what I am?"

"Chris, you know what I mean. You have always been charismatic, and for Lucy, it's appealing and new."

Chris smiled. "I like her. You don't have to wonder what she's thinking. It just comes right out of her mouth."

"Is that one of those backhanded compliments?" she asked cautiously.

"No, it's a sign that I'm tired of fighting on all fronts."

Lucy came back and delivered two large glasses of lemonade. Both of them picked up the glasses and clinked them together.

"I'm sorry I didn't have better news about what I've found so far in the books," she started.

"I know, but I should have figured there was something going on. This week has just been one blow right after another. I got you here to help, but there are conditions. My sister isn't happy with the project at all and is probably betting it falls by the wayside, and The Center itself is hedging that I'm going to sell it and use the land no matter how many assurances I give them."

"Your sister doesn't like healthcare? I would have thought, as a company, you'd be thrilled to get into it."

"Let's just say that this project is a personal mission more so than a money pot. My dad was an alcoholic that recovered, and I wanted to do something for him. My sister is not of the same mind."

Gina winced. "That sounds rough. It's never a good look when people you care about are at odds with you."

"What's funny is I thought she would change her mind over time."

Gina took another sip of her drink and studied him over the rim of the glass. "The two of you always look unified. I would have never guessed you had an issue at all."

Chris shrugged. "That's a part of being in the limelight all the time. You start to pretend everything is okay, and if not, it will become okay. You assume that the people around you will come to your way of thinking if you just wait."

"Well, that being said, I have to ask you, Chris. Do you want to do this health center? I can help you, but do you want to do this?"

"I do, and I want to be hands-on. I want to make something, Gina. I've torn things down and repurposed my whole career. This time I want to make it right and be a part of something."

"Okay, then you have to act like it."

Chris raised his eyebrows. "I put the money in, and I check on them."

"They don't need a cop to watch them. I need you to be involved in The Center and to work there. You need to be present, and just throwing money at it and then showing up every quarter won't cut it."

Chris stopped and looked at her. Gina hoped he found what he was looking for soon because she was trying her best not to fidget under his gaze. It wasn't just him looking. It was the intensity of his looking. As if there was nothing and no one else in the world. It unnerved her and sparked a tremor she wasn't ready to identify yet. Finally, she shifted in her seat, and it was as if that movement broke the spell.

"I'm saying," she blurted out, trying to break the silence that was hanging between them, "if you want the people to trust you at the site, you have to put in the consistent time. This may be your first healthcare venture but have some confidence in your sense. When you put in more, the others at the Center see that and they'll start to take you seriously."

Chris sighed and nodded his head. "You're right."

"What?" she sputtered.

"I'm saying you are right. I was trying to run this the same way I run my other businesses. I need to be more hands-on if I want to make this work. Thanks. I'm glad you can be honest with me."

"Honesty, I can do. I'm not sure you're going to want to hear it all the time, but I'll give you that."

He smiled at her, and she noticed the moment his gaze when from her eyes to her lips. She reflexively licked them, and his smile grew wider. "I'm hoping I'll be able to convince you on giving more than that."

She ignored his comment and took another drink of her lemonade so she could formulate an answer.

"Don't dream too big, Chris. Nothing has changed between us."

"I disagree."

Gina sat back in the booth. "Really? Well, let's hear it."

"A couple of days ago. I couldn't get you to stay in the room with me. Now, you're my fiancée—"

"In title only," she interjected.

"We're talking about being honest and open with each other."

"We need to if we are going to save this Center," she reminded him.

"And we're having lunch talking about each other."

Gina held her hand up. "Actually, you are talking, and I'm listening. It was the least I could do because you're paying for lunch," she finished with a smile.

Just then, Lucy came out carrying two burgers with mozzarella cheese, sweet potato fries, and an order of fried zucchini strips. Chris looked at Gina, and she knew she was smiling brightly.

"If you can't finish yours, I'll help you out because that's what I'm here for," she said with a smile.

Chris looked at the food and then at Gina.

"This is what you normally eat?" he asked skeptically.

"Yes, I'm a growing girl, and I have to fix big problems for corporations, so it takes a lot of brainpower. Eat up. Remember, you're going to be working side by side with me, so you'll need your energy. You know, to keep up."

Gina looked at Chris and smiled. She wasn't sure what was going on, but these moments of taking him by surprise would be few and far between. She was glad Lucy had brought the food out. It gave her some time to regroup.

This wasn't class, and she wasn't as sure as he was that she could handle Chris outside of a classroom.

$$Six$$

Gina knew the day was going to be challenging when her boss came to see her and it wasn't a working day, but that was the way her day was starting.

"Gina, a Miss Cora, is coming," Daisy said through the intercom.

Gina was no longer surprised by Daisy's front desk skills. She had found Gina an office this morning when she walked in, and it was completely furnished. As kind as Daisy was to her this morning, she had to wonder why Chris didn't have an office as well. Daisy had given her a choice of three offices, so space wasn't the issue. She put those thoughts to the side when she saw her boss, Cora Thalmine, standing at the door.

Gina watched the statuesque woman walk into the room and then take a seat. Cora had blonde hair that hung to her shoulders and then curled as if she had just stepped out of the salon. She was slender with a muscular build that still left her curves but made it obvious she worked out at the gym.

"Gina, how are you?"

"I'm good. Please, take a seat."

"So I have to tell you, yesterday was a first and very interesting for me. I received a very healthy check as if we had done a very large project for about three months with a full complement of project managers. Then Ms. Griggs sent over a contract saying it was a default payment for all of the problems Mr. Griggs may have caused. Then she let me know that you would be putting in for a leave of absence."

"It's complicated," Gina said. She hadn't meant to say a thing, but as Cora rattled off what had happened, Gina had begun to feel embarrassed and foolish. She had only been thinking about her and Chris and not what would happen at the consulting agency.

Cora let the silence build between them, and then she sat back in the chair and crossed her legs.

"I'm not here as your boss but as your friend. Would you like to tell me what is going on?"

Gina opened her mouth, but nothing came out of it the first couple of seconds. Then she closed her mouth and took a breath.

"Would you believe me if I told you nothing?"

Cora smiled. "No, I wouldn't, and I'd hope that you wouldn't insult either one of us with that answer."

Gina leaned back in her chair and slouched. "Okay, so you remember when I went to school last year?"

"Yes?"

"Well, I met Chris Griggs, but I didn't know it, and I thought we were starting a really…special relationsip, but then he turned out to be a tool and left. Now he's back, and he says he wants to try. Again."

Gina looked at Cora and saw she was still smiling and hadn't moved.

"You don't look surprised?"

"Well, when a man comes to my agency with a project plan and says he wants me to implement it. I am already suspicious by nature. When I read the plan, I was pretty sure it was your work."

Gina cocked her head to the side. "But you sent him two other project managers?"

"He didn't ask, and he paid to trial every one of the project managers. It was business. Now that he's paid me and you are on vacation, this isn't business, so don't let anyone tell you otherwise."

Gina shook her head. "No, no, it's not like that. He's not blackmailing me or anything. He's just…just—"

Cora held up her hands. "Since you seem to have a challenge talking today, why don't I ask the questions and guide this along?" she said, with laughter in her eyes.

"Are you two in a relationship?"

Gina squirmed in her chair. "I know this is going to sound odd, but we are not in a relationship, but we are telling everyone that we're engaged."

"Oh, this sounds like the beginning of a great story!"

"It just sounds that way."

"So, you care for him."

"I think he's got a good personality."

Cora laughed under her breath, "I suppose the fact that he's totally hot doesn't hurt either."

Gina looked over Cora's shoulder.

"I don't think we should say things like that here. I swear Daisy has ears everywhere."

Cora's eyes opened wide. "The interesting woman at the front? I wouldn't be surprised. I have to say being announced over the loudspeaker is a first for me. But that doesn't answer my question."

Gina threw her hands up. "Okay," Gina said, exasperated, "there is definitely some hotness to him. He's smart, and he's upfront now. I like talking to him, and he's got a way of being open to change without being offended by me. But the coup de grâce is he doesn't pause when he sees how much I eat."

"Then he sounds like a great catch."

"I have no idea if I want to catch him."

"The heart doesn't care. It doesn't look for the things we look for. I tell you that from experience. Give it a chance Gina."

Gina looked at her friend. "I think I'm scared to trust this."

Cora grinned. "If you're scared in a tingly kind of way and not a horror-show kind of way, go full-steam ahead and get ready for a ride."

"Give up my control and follow a man around? I can see that happening like…never!"

Cora stood up and smiled. "I came to make sure all was well. Call me when you're in a little deeper. Remember, your head may say never, but if your heart says otherwise, just hold on and prepare for the ride of your life."

Gina sat in her office with the light tones of classical music filtering through her headphones. She had bought the latest noise canceling headphones so she could find peace and quiet on any job. The music helped her to rest and clear her head. It was a mental reset. Gina felt like she needed it after the morning conversation with Cora. She had read her emails, and there was an announcement party being held tonight. Chris had come back tothe Center, but he had gone directly to his office, which she had asked Daisy to set up for him.

Gina imagined tonight's get-together would not be a pleasant event but a business one. It was being hosted by Julia Griggs, who wasn't known for her chipper disposition when it came to the New Hope Center. It was fine. Gina was going to take the time between now and tonight to ready herself.

The sound of the piano and strings playing in accord with each other and then lightly flowing to and fro were just what she needed now. She had a timer on her wrist to let her know she had indulged enough. Gina closed her eyes and her the cares float away.

She reflected on the last couple of days and found that she wasn't trying to forget them, but she was trying to accept and figure them out. Her inner project manager was glad that this was moving forward and that there would be some conclusion one way or another.

She felt a discordant vibration under her feet and opened her eyes.

In a moment, all the peace and calmness she had gathered was leeched from her as she saw the group standing in her office. Robin Craters, the Director of Operations—and the fundraiser for The Center if truth be told—came in and took a seat in the chair in front of her desk. She was now surrounded by her impromptu honor guard. Steve Langers, the Assistant Director of the children's program, and two other assistant directors, Clara Danford, who did outreach and assistant director Michelle Carlyle in charge of addiction services.

Gina took her headphones off, wrapped them up, and put them in the drawer. Then drawing a cleansing breath she no longer felt, she sat back and waited for the show to start.

Robin smiled and gave her a nod.

"We're glad we were able to catch you in the office, Ms. Key—"

Gina held up her hand. "No, please, it's Gina."

Robin nodded. "Gina. We've been meaning to get together so we could talk to you. First, we wanted to say congratulations and welcome to New Hope."

Robin was a solidly built woman at about five foot five at the most. She had black hair that had been cut into a bob and wore a white blouse with black slacks. Her neck was adorned with costume jewelry that had hints of onyx and opal stone in a metal disk. She reminded Gina of someone's aunt who came by to spoil you with cookies and vacations. However, there was no denying the mental acumen of the woman. When others had looked away, Gina knew Robin had raised money and saved the Center more than once.

"Hello, everyone," Gina said, "please forgive me if I don't address you all individually. It seems that you've caught me unawares. However, it's good to see you all."

"We would have had to find you no matter what if we want to save the Center," Steven murmured. Gina thought he was about five-nine. He had a fashionable beard that was brownish-red. His eyes were a startling blue and he looked fit in a white shirt and blue jeans.

Out of all the people here, Steven was the only non-clinical on staff. More than once, Chris had questioned his role, and in the documents, Robin had saved him more than once.

"Ms. Griggs has called a meeting," Steven blurted out. Gina could hear the tension in his voice. "The last time she called a meeting, it was to ask us to justify our positions. You can imagine her parties are not something anyone looks forward to," Steven continued.

"Tonight won't be about your jobs or having to justify them," Gina said, looking at the group. She could tell they were waiting, but Gina had no intention of answering any other questions. The thought of them deciding to come en masse might have worked with some people but not her. She was used to facing down CEO's and board members and delivering news that would make their bottom line tremble. She wasn't going to be intimidated by this group.

Michelle Carlyle stood with her arms over her chest. She was petite with blonde hair cut in a pixie style. If Gina hadn't heard Steven, she wouldn't know that Michelle was worried about anything. She had an elf-like quality that made her appear non-threatening to others. Dressed in a champagne blouse with a bow in the front and burgundy slacks, she appeared to be the epitome of calm.

Under Michelle's management, it appeared the enrollment rate had gone up, and the retention rate of the clients was up too. Michelle was one of the people who had first suggested that the Center directors should be given their own budgets to manage. Michelle had already complained to the Griggs that she should get a budget instead of having to go to Robin for funds. Gina couldn't name it, but there was something not quite right about Michelle.

Michelle took a step forward and offered her hand to shake. "So, how is it to work for the carpetbagger?" Michelle asked with a cocky grin.

Gina shook her hand and sat back in her chair. She couldn't say why at the moment, but she felt the need to defend Chris in his absence.

"I think you should rethink how you refer to him. I can only assume, since he's not running for office, that you are trying to ascribe the other meaning to him, which is unfounded as he is still pouring money into the Center with no return date in sight for the amount he's invested."

"It doesn't mean it's not going to happen," Clara muttered. "He's looking to get his money back by selling, and that takes time." If there was ever a living version of goldilocks, it was Clara. She had blonde hair that she kept back with a hairband. She wore a long dress that had pockets and looked more like an apron than a dress. She wore no makeup at all and no perfume to speak of. Clara was a community worker, and she was happy doing it. Everyone knew she despised the group meetings.

Robin cleared her throat, bringing the attention back to her. When Gina looked at Robin, she could see the tension in her face. According to the documentation, the answer was clear why Robin would be resentful. Robin had tried to run the Center and had only asked for assistance, but each time, a new owner came and decided to take over the Center instead.

"I can only assume Julia hasn't considered selling off any of the units to another center that would be willing to take them in," Clara asked impatiently.

Gina shook her head. "It's my understanding to broker a deal for one of the services would give the Griggs a negative return."

"The Griggs don't know healthcare, and they're trying to run this like a business," Robin stated. "They have to understand the industry and realize when people are involved, the rules are a lot more flexible. Did anyone tell them that? Maybe more importantly, now that you're here and helping your fiancé, do you know that?"

Gina smiled. She wasn't offended by Robin's forthrightness. She welcomed it. "I have made Chris aware of the nuances of the industry, and he'll be spending more time here so he can understand those nuances on a more personal level," Gina replied in a neutral tone.

"Well, it is very unexpected for you to show up and to be so prominent in this arrangement," Robin commented. "What is your intention here?"

There it was. Finally, Robin had asked. She wanted to know who would ask because it would let her know who the leader of the group was. She ignored the rest and focused on Robin.

"We will save this Center, Robin," Gina said. "I will make sure to keep you in the loop. I am by trade a project manager, so while this is challenging, I need you all to have a little faith in Chris."

Michelle sighed. "Have faith in the man who wants to sell the land and destroy the Center? He's just biding his time for a good bid," she murmured.

Gina focused on Michelle for a moment and kept that in the back of her mind. Michelle was the most openly pessimistic.

"I want you all to know that I am happy that we were able to meet, but I have some things to look over and plan. There is a get-together tonight and I need to get home to dress."

"Gina, I wanted to know if anyone had said anything about the children?" Steven asked.

Gina's gaze softened, and then she spoke softly to Steven. "Chris and I are definitely concerned for the children and they will be a part of the long-term plan."

She could see him take a breath and rest against the wall.

"Now, everyone, if you'd please."

They all rose and filed to the door when Robin turned back to Gina. "Oh, Gina dear, just one more thing. I wondered why Julia was giving the party if Chris is going to be taking care of things? Is Julia taking over?"

Everyone at the door turned in unison to hear the answer. She gave them all a smile and stood up. She held out a hand and herded them towards the door.

"I think we all have questions, and they will be answered tonight. I really don't have anything else to tell you."

"I told you it's only a matter of time before a good offer comes along that no one can say no to," Michelle muttered again.

"Please, until tonight." Gina moved forward and they all finally exited the door. When they were out, she leaned against the door and took a breath. She wasn't sure how she would get through tonight.

Seven

Her bell rang, and once again, she missed having a roommate. Natalie had left and gotten married and while Gina was thrilled, her friend was living in wedded bliss, it was so inconvenient at times like this.

She had a metal hanger in her right hand, and she put the dress over her head and pulled it down past her hips. The doorbell rang again. She shuffled to the front door, taking small steps so she wouldn't lose the whole ensemble.

"I'm coming!"

Her hair was already up, and she had decided to put on a little black dress. She could put a jacket with it and look corporate or take it off and look casual. All that planning would have been great if it wasn't for the fact that the zipper was in the middle of her back right below her bra clasp. She looked out the peephole, and sure enough, it was him. She pulled open the door.

"Get in, I need you," she said.

"If I had known I'd get this greeting, I would have come sooner."

"Don't get happy, it's not that kind of need." She turned to him brandishing the metal hanger.

Chris held his hands up. "Whoa, I get the hint."

Gina looked at the hanger and then tossed it on the couch. "No, I need you to zip me up."

"Ah, that I can do."

"I bet you can," she murmured.

When the zipper was up, she turned to look at Chris. He was dressed in a beige shirt and black jeans.

"Am I overdressed?" she asked.

Chris shook his head and perused her from head to toe. "No, you're perfect. This is a message to my sister."

"Did you want to talk about something?"

Chris took her arm and guided her to the door. When they were out, Gina locked it and then followed Chris.

"Why did you ask if I wanted to talk about something?"

"I have my own car, but you wanted to drive."

Chris opened the door to his black two-seater truck. "It wasn't that I wanted to talk, I thought we'd walk in together, being that we're engaged and all."

Gina looked at him as he got behind the wheel. "Did you tell your sister the truth?"

"The truth is that I'm working on it, and that wouldn't be the answer she would want."

"So much for honesty," Gina murmured.

"I fully believe in the principle that honesty is the best policy. However, I find I have someone very dishonest in the mix, and I need to address it."

Gina shook her head in disbelief. "Do you still believe that someone in the Center is doing something wrong, deliberately?"

"Yes, I do." Chris drove onto the highway, and within minutes they were at the Center. As they pulled up to the building, Gina faced Chris.

"What is it that you think they're doing, stealing money? Because if they are someone is hiding it very well," Gina countered.

"I'm not sure what is being stolen or how right now. What I can tell you is the books don't add up, and I'm not sure how it's leaving the Center. Is it leaving as medications or cash? I need to find out."

"You know the Center will never be able to survive this kind of suspicion."

"They won't have to. I'll address it in-house via a friend who I know can be discreet."

"They came to see me today, and they all seemed very dedicated to the Center. I don't think you should say anything until you know for sure. They already think today is going to be another firing night."

"I can't blame them; it was exactly that the last time my sister called."

"So, keep this to yourself."

"And why is that again?"

"Because you are establishing that you are the leader and turning in your people doesn't make everyone feel safe."

"And the diminishing returns on the financials?"

"We will work it out," Gina said as she exited the car.

He followed her to the door and down the hall. "I've noticed that when you want something, Gina, it's we. Is that a sign that—"

"That I want you to take a leadership role? Yes, and we're working on it."

Chris shook his head. "They don't want a leader, and they don't want me in their daily business."

Gina smiled. "You'll just have to convince them otherwise. I have it on good authority you know how to plan, so winning over this small group will be a no brainer."

If looks could kill, Gina thought Chris wouldn't have made it past the doorway. Everyone was in there and the anger toward Chris was palpable.

Along the wall there was a table with snacks on it and in the middle of the room was a table with a pamphlet at every seat. Julia was there dressed in black from head to toe. It was hard to tell if she was there for a meeting or a funeral.

"Everyone, please take a seat. Let's get the meeting over with, and then you can go on your way."

People grumbled, but they all sat down.

"What is the reason you've called this meeting?" Robin asked.

"After Larry being let go, there is no one else we can let go and still function," Michelle said.

Julia waited until everyone was done and reacted to no one. "If you will look in front of you, everyone will notice a pamphlet. This pamphlet is an acknowledgment from the department of health that they will be coming to do an audit on us if we can't submit the documents they are asking for."

Julia looked around the table and then went on. "Now, I'm unaware if you can produce the documents or not. What I will tell everyone in this room is this, this facility has been running at a loss for more than two quarters. From a business point of view that is enough to close the Center today. However, my brother oversees this project, and he will have the final say on when enough is enough. I also want everyone to know that when he stops working here, the Center will be repurposed, and you will have to find a new location to serve your clients."

Gina watched Julia deliver her news and then get up and leave the meeting. She didn't wait for responses or anything else. Gina was feeling a little jilted. She thought tonight was going to be about her announcing her engagement to Chris and how she'd be a new fixture in the office. When Julia left, if it were possible, the group seemed to become angrier with Chris.

Chris stood up and went to the doors that led to the garden. The faint moonlight bathed him in an ethereal glow, making him look like he was on the cover of a magazine. The others got up and went to the snack table, mumbling. Gina knew this was about crowd control. She would tell Chris later that he couldn't just separate himself, but right now the group needed to be rallied after the blow Julia had delivered.

"He doesn't care about the children, it was always about the land," Ryan said, shaking his head. "He was just biding his time after all."

"This is a community business. It's here to serve those less fortunate. So few of these Centers really exist, and it's because of big businesses seeing their pockets instead of seeing the people," Robin complained. "People shouldn't suffer because of the ignorance of a big business owner."

Chris turned around and faced the group at the table.

"You're right; a business needs someone who knows what they are doing. Healthcare isn't my forte, but it is my fiancée's. I could have sold this Center many months ago, but I didn't. So I don't think my dedication to the project can be questioned."

He turned back to the window alone. The others just continued to mumble complaints until it made Gina angry.

"He's played the game well," Michelle said, then she turned towards Gina.

"Are you going to be his justification for closing our Center? Do they give you a cut of the sale?"

Gina's lips pursed, and she closed her eyes, trying to bring back the harmonious sounds of her headphones.

"Michelle has a point, what do you get out of this Gina?" Robin asked tentatively.

"You can all stop right there," Chris said from the doors. His tone made everyone stop and give him their attention. "If you want to question me, fine. If you want to complain about things not going your way, it's your right. However, under no circumstances will any of you question Gina's commitment or loyalty to this project."

Ryan looked bewildered. "I think it's fair that we should know where everyone stands."

"There is no discussion on right or wrong, fair or not. Gina doesn't need to answer to any of you. She doesn't have to share where her loyalty lies. She doesn't work for any of you. In fact, on her whim, if she decides this project can't be done, she can end it all."

There was a silence in the room that made Gina uncomfortable. She thought Chris had done that to emphasize she was his fiancée, but it did feel good to have him defend her and give her that much authority, even if it was just for show.

"She'll be working in the Center," Michelle murmured.

"She'll be there as my eyes and ears, no one else's," he said softly. "I want those words to settle in. If you have any other questions or comments, email me, and I'll set up an appointment with you to address it. Gina, I believe this meeting is over."

Chris walked by everyone to the door, and just as Gina was turning to follow him, her arm was grabbed by Michelle.

"Obviously not now, but I'd like to talk to you later, alone," Michelle hesitantly.

Gina nodded her head. "Of course, drop in when you can."

"Thanks, Gina," she said, holding Gina's hand between her own. "You know we all need to work together for the Center."

Gina didn't need to turn to know he was at the door waiting for her. When she looked over her shoulder, she saw just what she suspected, an impatient Chris.

Well, this was definitely not the way I expected the evening to end, Gina thought as she grabbed her purse and jacket off the back of the chair. *Nor is this how I expected to exit from it.*

Eight

"That dinner brought new meaning to the term thrills and chills." Gina rested her head back on the headrest of the truck and let the gentle sway of the vehicle lull her into a peaceful mood. It was odd that she found herself again feeling bad for Chris and wanting to help him again. The mixed signals she got from her brain were almost as bad as the mixed signals from her heart. She wouldn't try to figure it out tonight. She just knew that she wouldn't be able to let Chris go home after the fiasco of the night.

"It was everything I thought it would be from my sister."

Chris quietly drove the truck the rest of the way to her house and then walked her to the door without a word. When she had put the key in the lock, she turned to him.

"Do you want to come in and eat some scraps with me?"

Chris grinned. "I can definitely say that no woman has ever asked me that one."

Standing at the door with it slightly ajar, Gina felt a thrill go through her. Was she inviting the wolf into the pen? There was an uneasy excitement that coursed through her. Instead of shaking it off, she embraced it and decided she would follow Cora's advice and see what would happen. "Are you coming in?"

"I would be honored to accept your invite. It's not often that I get invited to a meal where someone really wants me to attend."

"Really?"

Chris nodded. "I'm not moaning about it. I make money, and other people would like to spend it. When I get invited to dinner, I know I'm supposed to bring my wallet."

Gina let Chris in and then closed the door.

"Well, I have to tell you there is nothing in here you need your wallet for," she said brightly.

Chris stopped in front of her and then reached out to lightly caress her cheek. "That just means everything here is priceless."

Gina cleared her throat and took a step back. "Calm yourself, Romeo, you're getting scraps and conversation tonight, and that's it. If you're thinking something else, you can use the door now, and there'll be no hard feelings."

Chris stepped back and shrugged. "How can a man resist such an invitation? Lead the way to the scraps."

Gina nodded. She kicked off her shoes and then dropped her bag and jacket on the couch as she went to the kitchen. She heard Chris chuckle behind her.

"What's so funny?"

"You do realize you just left a trail of outer clothing to the kitchen? Are you going to change?"

Gina shook her head. "Don't tell me you're one of those people who have different clothes for everything and every occasion. I can cook in all of my clothes. If they can't get dirty in the kitchen, those are not the clothes for me."

They went into the kitchen, and she started to pull out Tupperware containers from the refrigerator. Gina also pulled down bread, a cheese plate, and several containers of flavored hummus. Chris sat at the table, and Gina topped it all off with a glass of seltzer water.

Gina watched him look at the array but he didn't move.

"I can see you're lost. Let me help you out."

"I'd appreciate it."

Gina made them both plates with a little bit of everything. They ate in silence. Gina made sure to keep Chris' plate full. She went through a plate before she realized the food wasn't disappearing from his plate anymore.

"Is there a problem? Did you want something else?"

Chris smiled and shook his head. "I have to tell you it never gets old watching you eat."

Gina licked her fingers in front of him. "I'm glad to provide the entertainment for you."

Chris cleared his throat. "No, please, I didn't mean that the way it came out. What I mean to say is that it's a pleasant surprise to be around a woman who will eat instead of picking at her food."

"There is never a good reason to let food go to waste," Gina said as she cleared the table. "Are you done?"

Chris nodded. He picked up the plastic flute glasses and took them into her living room. After throwing out the paper plates and wiping down the counters, she joined him on the couch.

"I've been avoiding this talk for a while, but if we're going to be able to work with each other, we need to clear the past and then go forward as we can." Gina sat cross-legged on her couch and faced him. She had to inch up her black dress, but she was still decent.

"This is a minefield of a conversation. I think the smart thing to do is to let you lead," he said, turning to face her.

Gina had geared herself up to defend her stance, so this turn around was unexpected, but she didn't protest the situation. Instead, she went straight into it.

"Do you know what's wrong with the Center?" she asked.

Chris was confused. "Wow, are we not going to talk about us at all?"

"Ironically, this is the same thing. The thing that is wrong with your Center is one of the things that was wrong with us."

"Poor planning?"

Gina frowned. "Chris," she admonished.

Chris sat back on the couch and let out a sigh. "Okay, Gina, tell me," he said wearily.

Gina looked at him and then reached out to touch his arm. "Chris, we can talk about this some other time."

"No, let's do this. It gets a little tiring to hear what I'm not doing or what I should be doing. Tonight my sister wanted to make it known she wasn't happy, and she sent that message clearly."

Gina let go of some of her anger and began to rub his arm. "I know this must not be the easiest time for you. Learning about the Center and everything. Healthcare is a different kind of business than others, and it takes some maneuvering."

Chris smiled and put his hand over hers. "Thanks for not just walking out the door with Julia tonight. I would have been disappointed, but I wouldn't have been surprised."

Gina took her hand back. "I think I might be insulted. You think I'd leave you there alone to face them?"

"I think everyone is here because I forced them to be here, or I manipulated the situation. Nothing has turned out to be the way I thought it would be, so at this point, I'm anticipating the worst."

"Chris, the problem is trust. You didn't extend yourself to reassure anyone tonight. You didn't try to make them part of the solution. You didn't even discuss the possible audit," she reminded him.

"Why would I? I already know—"

Gina reached out and put two fingers on his lips. "Shh, this is where you get into trouble. You have to give people a chance to participate in things that will affect their lives. You can't be the sole person to make the decision."

"We spoke about everything when we were in and out of class. I respect your opinion and your work," Chris protested.

"But in the end, you decided to leave?"

"I did it because my world is so different than yours. I was happy you wanted to be with me, but in my world facing the people and things I deal with, you wouldn't have the same man you had in class."

Gina gave him a sad smile. "You mean you decided what would be good for me and acted on it without talking to me first?"

"I thought I knew, and I wanted what was best for you. You are precious, cute, and smart, all at the same time."

"If you're going to be on both sides of any given relationship, what's the use for the other person to show up?"

"I'm just used to having to take care of everything. A democracy isn't the way it's usually done in business."

"I agree, but this is about people. People like to give their opinion when it concerns their lives as well." Gina sat back and folded her leg beneath her.

"You're right. It's a challenge for me," Chris said. "But, I'm trainable."

"Really?"

"I am. I can get a whole board of people to vouch for me," Chris said with a smile.

"Seriously, Chris. I was hurt. Now I feel like I can't trust you. I feel like you'd say whatever was necessary to get your way. It makes it hard."

"I want us to work Gina. You're good for me, and I'm hoping you're going to see something in me that's good for you too. I'll be honest and tell you that I need a little leeway when it comes to making decisions. I do it all day to make sure everyone is okay and that my family's future is safe, and it's been working."

Gina looked down and sighed. She had both legs beneath her now, and she just waited. He was right, but she wasn't willing to settle on this. She wouldn't just put her life and heart in the hands of a man who would always make decisions for them both.

"Stop, I can see you thinking so hard it's making me dizzy over here. Relax, and we will both figure this out," Chris said gently.

She looked at him skeptically. "Are you sure you even want to try this?"

"Oh, on that one, I'm completely sure. How it's going to execute though, I haven't made my four box plan yet."

"Four box plan?"

"It's a Griggs secret," he said with a smile. "I was wrong last time we were together. I looked at what you did but not why. Let's fix that. What are you doing at this company you work for? Looking to move up or open your own shop?"

Gina relaxed and gave him a shy smile. "I'm thinking that I like working for Cora. She's a friend and a boss. I still don't think I know enough about business yet to think about going on my own. Maybe now that I have this big time fiancé, I'll learn some things."

"Rule number one, don't hire family. They are the best and the worst. No matter what, they say, personal stuff always finds a way in."

"Well, I don't have any living family as it were, so I should be safe," Gina said.

"I'm sorry. I didn't know you were—"

"That I was free?" Gina said with a smile.

"Free?"

"Yes, free. I have been through several family living arrangements. One of the things I love right now is that I can come and go as I please."

"So let's see if I have this. One you want to learn some more before you maybe open your own shop. Two, you like your freedom, and I haven't heard anything about a significant other."

Gina grinned. "Are you trying to ask me what kind of guy I'm looking for? That seems a bit self-serving,"

"Oh no, it's completely self-serving. It's part of this new *let's ask everyone for information instead of just assuming we know* program."

She looked at him, and he seemed completely relaxed on the couch. His eyes seemed half-closed and his hands were folded on his lap. They were joking, right? This was crazy! She was having a grown-up theoretical conversation with a man, and she was as confused as if her high school crush had come by and asked if she wanted to go out on a date.

"In the interest of helping you, I'll answer. I am looking, at some point, to have a man in my life. I'm picky, and they would have to be able to deal with my eccentric habit."

Chris smiled. "Only one habit?"

"Don't get cheeky over there. I only have one habit that has ever concerned me. I do love my food. He has to like food; otherwise, we are going to be apart for large swaths in the day."

Chris laughed and rolled is hand to ask her to go on. "Okay, what else would this amazing man need to be able to do?"

"I didn't say he had to be amazing?"

"Here's a lesson for business. Always aim high. At worst, you will fall short but still be ahead of the rest of the crowd. At best, you'll get what you really want and be way ahead of the crowd. The other lesson is if you can't see it then you can't get it. So many people say they want to be rich or marry the perfect guy but can't explain how they want to make money or what the perfect guy is like. Then when neither one of those comes true, they wonder why. You need goals to make it. So let's go, if you want him, you have to be able to describe him."

It was so odd having this conversation with Chris. Although if she were honest, she'd have to say this was one of the many things she missed about him. How odd this was to her, to talk about what she was looking for in the perfect man, *to* the man pretending to be her fiancé?

"If all limits are off," Gina said slowly. "I'd want a man who would protect me."

"From what?"

"Everything silly."

Chris opened an eye. "Is there something you want to tell me?"

"No. I don't think he'd ever have to, but if it was needed, I'd like to know he could handle it. It's got to be someone I trust. Someone who I could consider my friend. But the most important thing for me would be someone who could plan and do project management like me."

"Project management?" Chris looked at her with an eyebrow raised, and eyes opened. "Why does it matter if he can do project management?"

"Well, when you do project management work all the time, it seeps into your daily life. One of the things that I hated growing up were the adults who were uncertain and couldn't stick to a plan much less make one. So my thought is if he can do a project plan, then there will be less chaos in my life."

"It's odd to me that you seem to talk about everything but chemistry and attraction. Tell me, Gina, does it matter that the two of you are physically attracted to one another?"

"It plays a part," Gina hedged.

Chris sat up and faced Gina. "I think it's more than a part," he said.

"You're entitled to your opinion."

Chris reached out, and Gina pulled back.

"A test, nothing more," he said.

Gina leaned forward, and Chris' hand cradled her cheek, and his thumb moved back and forth over the swell of her cheek.

"The placement of attraction being so low on the list leads me to believe we haven't explored this option fully."

Gina leaned into the soothing motion and sighed. "Oh no, I believe I've done my due diligence. A logical man who can plan and be my friend is going to win over my urges every day. Besides, when I find the right man, I'll find him appealing, not just his body or face."

"You know, Gina, when I told you I was going to need help with giving everyone a voice. Well, I'm about to backslide now into making the decisions for us all." That was when Gina opened her eyes and saw Chris's head coming towards her for a kiss.

Nine

Tonight was supposed to clear things up for Chris. Instead, his world was just getting murkier. He had gone tonight to ambush dinner by his sister, and now he was sitting with his pretend fiancée, who he really wanted to be his real fiancée, and was listening to requirements he wasn't even sure he understood much less had.

There was something that was good between him and Gina and there was low heat that was always being stoked between them. Gina was a force of nature and a breath of fresh air. She didn't take his crap. As far as Chris was concerned, she hadn't mentioned a single thing he could say he could check off the list as having. Then he pulled out the attraction card he could tell was always there between them.

As he was bending to kiss her, she opened her eyes. Of course, she opened her eyes. Gina wasn't a woman that things happened to. She was the woman that engaged in the experience. She always met him no matter where they were. He didn't expect this kiss to be any different.

His lips touched hers and it was with a sigh of relief that she stayed still and didn't pull away from him. Until that moment, there was a fear that she wouldn't remember this about them. When he saw the directors try to gang up on Gina he made a decision. He didn't want to just protect from the directors, he wanted to protect her from everything, forever.

The problem was Gina was taking great pains to let him know that they may not work out. Unless he could convince her otherwise. After her brushed by her lips once or twice, a small sigh escaped her lips and she relaxed into giving him more access.

His hand stayed on her cheek. He didn't trust himself beyond that. He inched a little closer to her so he could angle his head a little more and deepen the kiss. That move brought him knee to knee with her on the couch. His fingertips were tickled by wisps of hair that had come down at the nape of her neck. The smell of coco butter and something sweet wrapped itself around him and tempted him to lean in closer and take a deeper drink of the well.

Her movement gave him all the reassurances that they were connecting and both on the same page. When her lips moved and met him at every brush and turn, Chris could feel the victory song building in his spirit. This he could do. This he rocked at, and then he felt her hand on his chest. For a moment, he was ecstatic and overwhelmed that she felt comfortable enough with him that she would want to be closer. Then his senses came back online and he realized she wasn't pulling him closer but she was slowly pushing away.

He lifted his head, confused. Chris didn't understand what had happened. He was in the zone and he knew she was with him and then she stopped. It was worse than a blow to the kidney when she pulled back. He hoped that she just wanted to come up for air, he leaned down and her hand again stopped his descent.

"Chris? I think that's enough."

"You think that's enough," he parroted.

"Yes, I do. I'm not saying it wasn't pleasant."

"Pleasant?" he repeated.

"I'm just saying we need to keep a focused head and make sure we make informed decisions."

Chris sat back and looked around the room. "Yeah, informed decisions."

"Okay, come out of it, Chris. Don't act all shell shocked that I'm not in a ravenous state to explore the kiss. The kiss was good, but I told you, that's not the way to my heart," she smiled faintly. "Come on Chris, shake it off. You've still got it. Whatever *it* is. I just don't want it right now."

Chris sat back. "Don't sign up for the cheer-up squad because you're bad at it."

"Chris. I still think you're hot. I'm just not looking at hot now."

"And what are you looking at now?" he asked dejectedly.

Gina reached out and cupped his cheek. "I'm looking for a friend."

"There's nothing wrong with being a friend and indulging in the sweeter sides," he said with a wan smile.

"This time, we're going to go slow for me. I'm not interested in a quick fly by night thing. If I'm going to do this, then I want to do it right and be sure. Right now, I'm not even sure we can do friends."

"Why, because I'm not a project person?"

"I won't kid you, that project thing is really important," Gina added on. "Maybe we should stop while we are ahead and call this a night."

Chris wanted to argue, but he didn't know what to say and so for once, he did what was suggested and he stood up and went to the door.

"Are you okay?" Gina asked.

Chris smiled. "I'm good, not happy, but good. We'll do this your way Gina, but don't hold it against me when I throw in a wrench or two."

They were at the door and Gina was standing barefoot in a little black dress seeing him out.

"You can try Chris but I'm ready for you." Chris tipped his imaginary hat at Gina and then left.

Ten

Gina waited on pins and needles the next day. She wasn't sure if Chris would come into her office or not. Her nerves were about shot when the knock came to her door and in walked Michelle.

"Hi, Gina, do you have a moment?"

Gina nodded, and Michelle came in. Michelle had that slow walk about her as if she were trying to find the words to say what needed to be said. Gina had seen this slow gait on many a person right before they had to deliver bad news.

Michelle settled down and then smiled. "I want to thank you for seeing me. After last night I wasn't sure if I would be welcome."

"Business happens all the time. We have to be able to roll with the punches and carry on."

"I'm so glad you feel that way, Gina." Michelle appeared to relax a little in the chair. Gina was just waiting for the other shoe to drop.

"What can I help you with, Michelle?" Gina said, hoping her smile was firmly in place and conveyed just the right amount of friendliness.

"Well, things had been hectic at the Center before you came, and there have been some things that just had to be done. I didn't want to do them, but the people are what is most important, you know? But now things are changing, and I think that Griggs is really going to help people, and that changes everything."

Gina let Michelle ramble. She didn't interrupt her. Gina could tell that Michelle had needed to say whatever she was trying to say for a while. When Michelle was done, Gina began.

"So, I can see that you're distressed and you've made a decision. I want thank you for telling me. However, it is my experience that, all that rambling usually means one of two things: something is missing, or money is needed."

Michelle's smile disappeared, and her head fell into her hands. "Both!"

Gina looked at the distraught Michelle and pulled open her drawer. "This is definitely a candy bar moment." Gina pulled out a chocolate bar from her drawer. She had cut it into four sections. She usually kept a sweet in the office, and this counted as four sweets even though it was one bar. "So, what is the possibility that you could just tell me the damage?"

Michelle nodded. "I can. What happened was—"

Gina nodded as Michelle began the story and pulled out a second piece of the candy bar. It was always like this. She just wanted to know the end of the story so she could try to fix it, but people always wanted to explain as if it made the troublesome end result okay.

Michelle sniffed and started in on her story.

Gina held up her hand. "Just tell me the trouble part."

"The trouble part is eighty thousand dollars and the Center is closed."

Gina opened the drawer and pulled out the third piece of candy. "I really hope you are given to exaggeration."

"I'm sorry, I'm not." Michelle stood up and began to pace in the office. When she looked at Gina, there were unshed tears in her eyes. "I was trying to help people who couldn't help themselves. When I did an old employee, Larry Wakefield, the old nurse, found out and now he wants medications or money. So I've been giving him money until I find an answer."

"You've got eighty thousand sitting around?"

"No."

"Then it seems we are out of options, and we need to learn something from this."

"Yes?" Michelle said.

"We don't pay blackmailers because they are never satisfied."

Michelle flinched from Gina's tone. "I can see there is a lesson in this but for right now, to make sure the Center is okay, we need to find the money to give to him!"

Gina popped the first piece of chocolate into her mouth. "You know, Michelle, if I had eighty thousand dollars, I wouldn't give it away." Gina rolled the chocolate cube in her mouth and savored the rich taste on her tongue.

Michelle stopped pacing and then looked at Gina. "You could ask for that kind of money from your fiancé."

Gina stopped chewing and started straight away unwrapping the second cube of chocolate.

"I can see how you might think that's an option, but it's not," Gina said firmly.

"It can work! I could help you make up a starter plan, and he'd give it and then—"

"I don't know if I should be insulted or not. I'm not sure what makes you think Chris would just give me the money but—"

"Last night made me think about it. He's been to those meetings, and his sister always fires someone, or we all complain. Last night he defended you to the rest of us and then left. You are the new piece here. For you, Griggs would do it."

"I don't take money from Chris. I would never allow money to be a part of our relationship."

"You don't have to keep it, just loan it to me, and I'll pay it back once we figure out—"

Gina held up her hands. "Stop, just stop. I will not ask Chris for the money." Gina cleared her throat. "I'll ask for his advice, but we will both have to wait to find out what can be done."

Michelle took a seat in the chair. "How can you be so calm?"

Gina popped the second candy in her mouth. "I don't move without a plan, and I don't get flustered by incoming drama. I expect it."

Gina was debating putting the third piece back into the drawer when her door opened.

"Gina, let's do lunch and discuss some things, I…wanted…to. I'm sorry, am I interrupting?" Chris asked.

His timing would have almost been funny if the situation hadn't been so serious. Michelle looked like she had been caught with her hand in the cookie jar.

Chris looked at Gina liked he was waiting for an explanation, and Gina put the third piece of chocolate back into her top drawer and pulled out her handbag from the bottom drawer.

Gina did the only logical thing. She smiled at Michelle. "Michelle, why don't we continue later. I'll reach out to you, but until then, do nothing."

Michelle nodded and then scurried out of the door past Chris. When Michelle was gone, Gina cleared her throat to get his attention.

"So you mentioned the food and now you've got my attention and my stomach. I haven't eaten yet, and my pit is empty, so I hope you brought deep pockets."

Chris watched Michelle leave the room and knew he had walked into something.

"Did you want to talk about that?"

Gina shook her head. "No, not really. Where are you taking me?"

Chris took her to his place. He imagined that his place must look almost sterile to her. He had a cleaning service come in once a day and make sure everything was in its place. Chris recalled seeing her leave the trail of clothes and couldn't ever remember seeing his own clothes anywhere but in his closet or going out the door in a basket.

He'd had a revelation.

Gina was the one.

He'd been up all night trying to figure out how to woo his fiancée. He had a large living room with a small couch and a respectable theatre screen for the television. It opened to a dining room area that was already preset with food.

"You cooked for me, so I thought I'd return the favor," he said.

Gina took off her coat and dropped it on his couch and then continued to the dining room. It took all of his self-control not to pick it up, but he supposed this was a small thing when it came to being with Gina. By the time he looked up, she was already pulling out a chair and sitting at the table.

"You cooked this?"

Chris shrugged. "I paid for it, so that's the same difference."

"Whatever, sit down already" she insisted.

Chris sat down, and then she interrupted his thought.

"Chris, what's wrong?"

"I had a plan, and it all went to crap."

Gina reached for the platters of food and started serving them both.

"Tell me this plan of yours?" she asked.

"I was going to take your bag or coat. Then I would pull your seat out and—"

"And I'm curious, would you do any of this for Tim?"

Chris stopped cold. "No."

"Then, why me?"

"You're my fiancée and—"

"But it's just us, Chris. Here with us two, I'm not your fiancée. I'm here for the Center, and we talked last night. So I'm not clear what your—very skimpy plan, by the way—was supposed to do?"

Chris was silent and all of a sudden, what he had hoped to be a romantic lunch, had become a mess. He heard Gina push her chair out, and he stood at the same time.

"Gina, please stay," he said, holding out his hand.

"Why?" She sounded hurt, and it killed him to know he was the cause.

"Stay because I'd like to get to know you."

"Chris—"

"As a friend."

Eleven

How did he know all the right things to say? She could tell this wasn't what he was expecting, and she wanted to comfort him. He couldn't know that him trying was just making her fall deeper in love with him.

"Let's start over," he asked.

Gina grinned and nodded. She got her bag and went to the door.

"Hey," he reached for her.

"Calm down, we're starting over to see if you can get it right," she said with a grin. Gina stepped out of the door and then opened it again. When she opened it, he had just made it to the living room.

"Hi Chris, you shouldn't leave your door open. You probably have a lot of expensive things in here."

Chris blinked as if he were shell shocked. "Wow, at this rate, you might be one of my slower friends," she said as she dropped her bag on the couch and went to the table.

Chris looked between her and the couch. "Slower friends? I am not slow. I just can't believe how messy you are."

Gina smiled, and Chris made it to the table. "I have to be messy because I save all of my organization for my work. That's why companies pay me good money."

He started digging into the food, and the tension that had been in the air before was gone.

"So this friend thing—" Chris started.

"Yes?" Gina laughed. "You make it seem like you don't have any."

"Well, I don't really. I had work from the time I was in high school. I always had a summer job at the company, and when the hard times came, and my dad couldn't always perform, I was there. So, business associates, I know how to work with. Friends? And ones that look like you? Not so much."

"Well, let's shake on it." Gina held out her hand. "Hi, friend."

She watched him look at her hand. "Friend?" she said, hand extended.

Chris picked up a napkin and shook her hand. "Friend."

"You've got to be kidding me. I thought the house was just clean from a maid. You mean you're really this clean? This much cleanliness is a cry for help."

When they had finished eating. Chris took her back to the office. She had just stepped inside, and he was in the doorway.

"I want to thank you for lunch. It was unexpected, fun, and definitely better at someone else's place," she said with a smile.

He was still standing there. She could see him looking at her lips, and then he closed his eyes and took a deep breath.

"Yeah, friend, it was great. There's a seminar tomorrow. Clara and Tim were invited to it as well. It's when all the similar sized Centers talk strategy. The more friends, the better," he said finally.

"You're doing great, Chris."

He nodded and then left. When the door closed, she leaned her head against the wall. She should be happy. They were friends. She had time to assess what she was feeling for Chris with no pressure.

All of that was true. Gina thought about how close his mouth had been from hers. She thought about how Chris couldn't hide his hitched breath or smoldering gaze. Oh yeah, they were friends. This would be just fine. Famous last words.

Convention Centers always managed to harness the best of the city. The Upper Valley Convention Center was no different. It offered a spectacular view of New York City from one side and a forest reserve on the other. Gina was at the top of the Center on the fourteenth floor. The meet and greet was going on downstairs. She didn't want to be in that crush and have to face odd questions. Instead, she came up here to relax, hear herself think, and try to work out the issues the Center was having.

Gina heard someone clear a throat behind her. It was her bad luck, Gina had come to get away from everyone and it sounded as if Clara had found her and was about to disturb her peace. "Is there any word on what Chris is doing? I know you care about the Center. You're the first one to care."

Gina sighed, "I thought we all came here to listen to the seminar?"

Clara shifted from foot to foot. "If Chris came to this seminar, it's because he needs information about something. I need you to think about the Center and what's best for us all."

Gina was a little tired of everyone saying she needed to think about what was best for the Center.

"Look, Clara, I'll let you know if there is anything you can do to help. Right now, I'm fixing the plan and checking the resources."

Gina watched Clara's face go blank when she talked about resources. She kept that in her pocket.

"Steven gets along with everyone, and he says Chris isn't a team player. Clara stood by Gina and looked at the landscape. "Be careful, Gina. Don't let your guard down just because you think you are working on the same goal."

Gina cleared her throat. "As his fiancée, letting my guard down is my everyday state. Clara, I know Chris can seem aloof and odd, but it's because he's still trying to get his business rules to merge with healthcare." Gina didn't know what else to tell her and got ready to leave when Clara called out.

"Gina?" Gina turned back to Clara.

"We all want to work as a team. To do that, we all need to know what it is that Chris is doing, you understand?"

Gina shook her head and let out a breath. "It seems to me that if you didn't have something to hide, you wouldn't care what Chris was doing."

Clara looked away from Gina. "We all have to live with ourselves, Gina. I hope you can be more open minded about our challenges. We want to be here for the community, and its hard when the only thing people see is a great piece of land."

"I hear you, Clara, but it doesn't really matter to me. I'm Chris' fiancée, which pretty much means my loyalty is to him first."

"I hope that our working together won't be harmed by my past with Chris?" Clara said.

It took everything Gina had to keep the serene smile on her face.

"Of course not, Chris is with me, so I don't worry about anyone in his past."

Clara nodded and smiled. "Chris is a good person, and I'm sure you two will be happy."

"Thank you." Gina could feel the smile starting to hurt.

"Ladies," Chris said from the door. He gave Gina a second look and then continued. "The seminar is about to start. Tim already has our seats."

"Well, I'm more than ready to move on," Gina said, and Clara rushed out the door.

Chris looked at Gina. "What's up?"

Gina walked up to him and poked him in the shoulder. "I think we need to go over some things that friends usually share, like your last girlfriend."

"Girlfriend? Oh, you mean Clara?"

"Yeah, Clara! You would think you'd give me a heads up since I'm your fiancée and all."

"It wasn't that way."

Gina held up her hand. "It doesn't make a difference what way it was, this isn't real between us either, right friend? I'll see you at the seminar."

Gina didn't wait for his response but went to the seminar room. When she got there, she scanned the room and saw Tim in the fourth row from the back of the room. She wasn't happy to see him, but right now, he was preferable to Chris. She was feeling fifty ways to stupid.

He was missing her, he had said. He had left because it was the best for them he had said. In Gina's head, she was going over all of the stories he had told, and they were just adding up to artful lies. What was worse was that she was hurting. Hurting because she thought, she thought it was going someplace else, and now it looked like…well, she didn't even want to think about what it looked like. Gina just needed to get through the seminar.

Tim sat down next to her, and Clara sat on her other side, leaving Chris to sit on the other side of Clara. When she took her seat, Tim smiled and handed her some pamphlets.

"This might not be the most interesting seminar. It's on supply management. Are you sure you wanted to be in this one?"

"I'm here because Chris thinks this would be great for us all to attend."

"I guess so, since as his wife, you'll be involved in his daily activities in the business. Daisy has taken a liking to you. I know we haven't had a chance to really talk did you want to have lunch? It's usually something boxed, but we can get our box and eat in peace?"

Gina looked at Tim and smiled. She hadn't expected an offer like this from Tim but right then it sounded wonderful. "I think that would be a great idea."

"Good, I'll meet you outside of this room when lunch comes, and we can sneak off then."

Gina laughed and then bent over to pick up the program pamphlet on the carpeted floor. When she sat back, her gaze locked with Chris'. Mr. Lothario was not pleased. *He probably thought he would go out with me for lunch to explain his other friend.*

Gina didn't even want to dwell on it now. Going to lunch with Chris right now wouldn't have been productive at all. Even though she knew that was the truth, when she sat back and listened to the presenter, Gina she didn't feel the satisfaction of doing what was right. It seemed that the only thing she knew for sure was that Chris Griggs was driving her crazy!

Twelve

"Griggs seems like he is really starting to get into gear since you came," Tim said at lunch.

True to his word Tim was waiting outside of the seminar room with two cardboard boxes. He lifted them up into the air, and Gina smiled. Tim found an empty conference room, and they sat there to eat.

Gina opened up the bland box and sighed. She should have known that Tim would make his pitch as well. It was only because she had been so distracted by Chris that she found herself in this position in the first place. Inside the box was a turkey sandwich, a ginger ale, and a snack pack of nuts. Gina didn't think this could be any more depressing.

At every seminar before this meet, people had been cornering her to find out if Chris was going to finally sell the land or if he was going to revamp the Center into something for a more upscale residence. She had hoped this lunch would be a relaxing moment away from all of that. Now she was stuck with someone else who wanted to know if she knew what Chris was going to do and faced with a box of food that was a snack at best and a tease at worst.

"Chris does what he thinks is best," Gina said as she moved the sandwich and nut pack around as if she would find some other food in the box.

"Daisy says he's changing."

Gina let another sigh escape her lips. She looked up, and Tim was waiting for her to answer. She shouldn't hold it against him. She imagined that at his age and place in life, he was just as concerned with how he would make ends meet.

"I can't speak to his changing, but I can tell you that he is putting in a lot of work to make sure that he gives the Center the best chance it has for success."

"Come on, I know you two are newly engaged, but you must talk about business sometimes?"

Gina laughed. "Business? I try not to."

Tim shrugged. "I'm old but not dead. You young kids always manage to include money in every conversation. I've been at the Center for eighteen years. The last six years have been the roughest. I'm just thinking that you could help me and Daisy out, if you get a heads up is all."

"Really, Tim, I don't have anything else to say besides what I've already said."

She could see Tim open his box and pull out a sandwich. He didn't look too thrilled with it either.

"Well, I guess you kids may have other things on your minds like a wedding and all. I tell you if he has any money sense, he'll sell the Center."

"Who knows?" Gina added, opening up the nut packs and picking out a raisin or two.

"Griggs owns Chymera. They always sell stuff and make money," Tim said. "It was odd for him to buy this place anyway, and no one expected him to hold on to it this long."

"Healthcare is big. I'm surprised you're so negative," Gina said.

"It's about money, young lady. It's always about money. Jobs are hard to do. Hard to come by as well. Just think about it Larry Wakefield who used to work here. He was the old head nurse. He's been hanging out with Clara. I guess he's hoping he can get his job back. He considered himself a ladies man at the clinic."

"I wasn't aware that Larry was still around or that you still talked to him," Gina said as she put down the plastic container.

Tim nodded and took a bite of his sandwich.

"No one knows what is going on so we all have to hold on to old and new contacts. Besides, if the Center doesn't go under then there might be a job for Larry again. Why do you look so shocked?" Tim asked.

Gina shook her head. "I thought he would have moved on."

Tim put his sandwich down and looked intently at Gina. "Listen, I hope you consider telling me if any major changes are coming. If not for my sake, then think about Daisy. We could sure rest easier having someone on our side."

Gina's appetite was gone and watching Tim vigorously eat the sandwich was killing any hope she had of eating. She wondered if there was anyone else left to make a pitch to her to find out what Chris thought about things. She wanted to make sure there was no conflict, so she was posing as his helpful fiancée, but she didn't think that would qualify her as the weak link to be pumped for information.

The back door opened and in stepped Chris.

"I'm sorry to disturb you but I wanted to borrow my fiancée, Tim," Chris' words were playful, but there was an intensity in his stare and stance that put Gina on alert.

"I'm coming."

Tim looked over his shoulder and then at Gina. "You want me to—"

"No, thank you Tim. Thank you for lunch."

"Oh, leave the box I've got it. You know we've got to be there for each other."

Gina nodded and then went to Chris. He put his hand on the small of her back, and she went to the door with him.

"I have to know, is this the way we solve problems? You find out information, and then you don't give me a chance to explain?"

"It's amazing to me that you can have this conversation as we're walking through the seminar hall," Gina said sarcastically.

"I might not get another chance because my friend is giving me the cold shoulder."

Both of them were stopped by a politician who wanted to congratulate them on saving the Center. They both smiled, and then Chris escorted the two of them into his truck.

Chris started driving.

"Okay, friend, where are we going?" Gina asked.

"We're talking. There was nothing between Clara and me. A couple of coffees does not make a relationship."

"Coffee?"

"Yes, coffee and maybe some strudel as well, but that's it."

Gina looked at him and then out the window and said nothing. "Friends are honest with one another so I'll tell you, I was a little miffed when she said that, but that was just washed away by the way I was just taken in by Tim. He was trying to pump me for information, and I just walked right into it."

Chris pulled the truck over to the side of the road and looked at Gina. "So, you didn't go to lunch with Tim to get back at me for Clara?"

Gina gave him a raised eyebrow. "No, Chris. I was upset, and he just asked me. Besides, if I were going to do that, and I'm not saying I would, I think I could find a better guy than Tim."

Chris laughed. "You're right, you could. I was just—"

"Jealous?"

Chris shook his head. "I was scared if you want the truth. I thought I had just started to get this right, and now it was going to crap over coffee."

"Friends are honest with each other and don't play those games. Unless I tell you that is what I'm doing."

"How does that make sense?"

"It's about disclosure," Gina explained.

Chris laughed. "I think I know why I don't have a lot of friends."

"Why?"

"The rules make no sense!" Before Gina could respond, he held up his hand. "How about we end on a good note, and I take you somewhere that involves food?"

Gina's eyes lit up. "There might be hope for you yet with this friend thing. Let's go!"

Thirteen

Chris watched Gina's eyes pop open as if it were Christmas when he brought her to the chocolate shop. As soon as they opened the door, he could smell chocolate in the air. He'd found the spot by accident in Queens and thought it would be a great place to take her.

He'd come by the day before to see if he needed an appointment. When they told him he could walk in, he was sure that after the seminar he could start to woo Gina from friend to fiancée here. Then the whole debacle with Clara happened, and he couldn't even think straight when he saw her with Tim. Even he had to take a second thought. Was he really jealous of Tim? That was just a wake-up call that what he was feeling wasn't going to go away.

"Would you look at that?" Gina said pointing toward the ceiling" "I think the pipes are filled with chocolate! And look, they have three chocolate waterfalls on that table."

Chris followed behind her and watched her go from chocolate fountains to display cases full of different chocolate cubes. When she had finished taking it in, he tapped her on the shoulder.

"The chocolate isn't going anywhere, let's have a seat and you can have them bring chocolate to the table."

"Are we here too early for food," she asked. They sat down in a red U-shaped love seat. It left no room for personal space and for a moment, Chris thought Gina would protest, but she settled down and waited in anticipation.

"No, we are the first ones here, but they're open. If they weren't, I'd have them open it for you," he said as she pulled the chocolate squares that were set as freebies on the table toward her.

Gina smiled. "Well, it seems that you want me in a good mood."

"I always want you in a good mood, but it's true, I thought this place would fix a couple of things at one time."

"Well, let me commend you on your attentiveness to know I like chocolate, but I wouldn't have let you open it just for me. If it had been closed, we would have had to go back to the seminar."

"Gina, it's a store. I've got the kind of money that makes store owners love to open for me. It increases their bottom line for the next seven days, at least."

Gina popped the last square on the table in her mouth and then sat up. Chris could see her mentally and physically getting herself together to fight. He didn't think she'd be so skittish. In fact, he had been hoping the "Chocolate Spot" would have soothed her.

"This is a bit much for friends," she said.

"Chocolate?"

Gina sighed. "You know what I mean." She opened her arms and gestured to the surrounding place. "All of this."

"Ah, yes, well in the vein of honest friends, I'm working on something a little more than friends."

"We just had a fight. Don't you think you're moving a bit fast?"

"We didn't fight. I didn't tell you something. You gave me the cold shoulder. I got scared that I had lost you. I figure that if I can be scared to lose you, I may be past the point of friendship."

"But am I Chris?"

That was the question that was keeping him up at night. "I'm hoping that I haven't done something so bad that I've lost the woman who stood toe to toe with me when she believed she was right. You look like the woman who I've heard has been putting in a good word for me with everyone. Telling them I'm not the money-grubbing snake they think I am."

Chris leaned his head down, so they touched foreheads. "Tell me, Gina, am I moving too fast?" he whispered.

"I want you to be sure, Chris."

"Yes, Gina."

"You know I'm not like a lot of women. I don't eat salad. I talk in low, hushed tones. I say what's on my mind."

He brought his hand up to caress her cheek. "These are sounding like fine things for a woman to have." With each swipe, she seemed to relax a bit, and her breath was deeper and calmer. "Whatever it is, we can work on it together."

"I'm scared, Chris, and I can't believe we are having this conversation in public."

"Stop trying to distract me. Besides, you should admit these conversations should always happen where you are the happiest. That's why we're here."

"Ah, a man who plans. You get big points for that."

"So I've heard."

Chris leaned down and kissed the cheek he had just been caressing. The kiss was light and quick. Then he whispered in her ear. "Gina, I want you just the way you are."

When he pulled back, he could see the hint of moisture she tried to blink away. "Okay, but remember you asked for this."

"I'll remember."

Gina turned and leaned back into him and then raised her hand. "Chocolate, we need some chocolate here."

Three hours later, Chris pulled up to Gina's apartment. It was no wonder she had fallen asleep. She had eaten so much chocolate and food that she had waddled out of the chocolate spot with a smile on her face. She was curled up in the seat next to him. He reached out and tucked a piece of her hair behind her ear. This was what his future looked like.

It was different than when it was just him and his sister. Julia was something else he would have to address, as well. Right now however, when he thought about family and the future, Gina's face came to mind first.

Watching her enjoy herself was a joy in itself. Chris had been afraid to embrace this feeling the first time he had met Gina. He wouldn't make the same mistake twice. Now that he knew he could be complete, he was going to fight for it.

Gina would never be boring. He would do whatever it took to make sure she was happy. His mind thought over the Center and the problems he found in the books. He'd gotten the reports and all of it seemed to be correct. He understood business. It was black or white. That didn't mean Gina was going to understand. She was methodical, but she also had a soft heart.

"Chris, are we there?" Gina's voice was soft with sleep. She snuggled up on her side of the truck.

"Yes, we're here."

"Good, I think I want to sleep another hour before I get some dinner," she said.

Chris smiled. "I'm going to head to the Center and look over some things."

Gina reached out to him and patted him on the arm. "It's going to be okay, Chris. You'll figure out what's wrong. I know you will."

"Really?"

"Yeah"

"Thanks, but don't put me on too high a pedestal. I'll find I might not be able to get down."

Gina laughed and then sat up. "You can say whatever you want, but I know you can do this. When we were in school, you always started with a *we can do this* kind of attitude. You don't fail, Griggs."

Chris leaned over and kissed her softly on the lips. "You know, there was a time when winning was the most important thing, but recently that has all changed. Now, fixing the Center is great, but there are some things that are non-negotiable. Just so we're clear, Gina. The Center is important, but if I see it's taking a toll on you in a negative way. I'll close the Center and sell the land."

"What?" Gina caught his gaze and reached out to touch his cheek. The feel of her hand on his skin was like silk brushing against him. "You can't be serious."

"I am serious Gina." He looked deeply into her eyes, hoping his intent was showing through and she understood how important she was to him. "You're more important to me than this project, or the Center."

"You're cute, but you're crazy."

"Think what you want, but I want to make sure that I'm being transparent. Now come on, let's get you into the house."

They went to the door, Gina opened it and turned to Chris.

"So, thanks so much for lunch and the chocolate."

"Just to be transparent, I'm going to kiss you now," he said. "If you're not interested, here would be the time you say so."

When she said nothing, he took a step forward and cupped her face. As he leaned down, he could hear her breath coming faster. Her eyes were wide open as he lowered his head. He saw her tongue run over her bottom lip, and a slight tremble went through her.

He'd been looking forward to this all night, and now that it was here, he was the one who was nervous. Moments before their lips touched, he closed his eyes and gave himself over to the feeling of the moment.

Her lips were soft and welcoming as he brushed his over hers. He moved slowly over her mouth and picked up hints of chocolate. When he pulled back, he could feel her breath fanning his lips.

"Gina?"

"Yes?"

"Good night."

"What?"

He pulled back his hands and stepped away. "Good night Gina. I'll see you in the morning."

He dropped his hands and walked back to the car.

"Chris!" Gina called out.

He turned and looked at her.

"I just want you to know. That was almost as good as chocolate."

Chris smiled. "I can't ask for more than that."

He got in his truck and smiled all the way back to his place. There was some doubt before, but not now. He was sure. Gina was the one.

Fourteen

"I didn't expect to get a call from you," Cora said as she walked into Gina's office. Cora was all smiles as she took a seat. She glanced around the walls and looked ay all the plans and whiteboards. "Well, whatever the issue is, it can't be the project because I can see you have that under control."

Gina got up and locked her office.

"This must be serious."

"It is," Gina said, staring at her friend.

"Okay, spill it."

"The whole thing with Chris and me. You were right. We don't get to pick who we love," Gina told her.

"I take it something has happened, so you know for sure that he's the one?"

"Yes, we had a great time together," Gina said, thinking back on yesterday.

"So, you've chosen Chris?"

"Yes."

"Then what's the problem? Too much money? Looks too good?" Cora counted off with a smile.

She waved off Cora's statements. "You know I don't care about his money or his looks. Well, I care about the looks but not like that. It's the second time around for us and he left the first time. I guess because it feels so good this time, I have to wonder if I'm being desperate or stupid to give in to this, this time?"

Cora reached out and touched Gina's hand. "There are a lot of things I'd call you, but stupid isn't one of them. I can't say desperate would come to mind either. What I can say is you are the smartest person I know. You said it with different words, but you hit the issue right on the head. You're asking me if you should trust him with your heart."

Gina closed her eyes and let her head fall onto their hands. "Trusting myself into his care. What fool does that after the man in question has done wrong?"

Cora smoothed her hand over her head and then tapped her on the shoulder. "Why did you call me here? You've already mapped out the issues, pros and cons. I'm here to support you, not to make the decision for you."

Gina looked up into Cora's comforting face. "I don't want to be hurt, but I don't want to miss out."

"Let me tell you something. Once upon a time, I loved with all of my heart. I gave a man my heart unconditionally, and then we lost a child. The pain of that loss will be with me forever, but not a day goes by that I regret that love, for him or the child."

Gina sat up and nodded. "Okay, I'm going to do this."

Cora smiled. "I'm sure the man in question will be very happy."

"Maybe I should start to look at how he lives and be a little more—"

Cora cut her off. "No, Gina. Deciding to change the way you are just to fit into his world is another way to avoid trusting him. If you don't show your true self, then you can't really get hurt."

"What are you suggesting?"

"I'm not suggesting, Gina. I'm telling you. If you want to do this right and not try to sabotage this relationship, then you need to just be you. Besides, if he's been with you for longer than ten minutes, he's seen the true you already."

"Cora, what am I thinking?" she said as she put her hands on her cheeks.

"You're thinking way too much is the problem. Breathe, you've got this. Trust yourself, Gina, you are an amazing woman. Now, I'm going to go pick a charity to go to."

"Oh yes, I know how much you love those," Gina joked.

Cora looked skyward. "Yes, like a dentist visit."

"Cora?"

"Yes?"

"Thank you for coming."

"I wouldn't have missed this chat for the world. The best to you and your beau."

"Thanks, he'll need it," Gina said with a smile.

It was the afternoon meeting, and Chris was in her office looking at all the whiteboards she had put up regarding the plans and processes for the Center.

"I'm impressed you were able to narrow it down like this. I mean, I had seen it before, but these details weren't apparent," Chris said as he looked over her work.

Gina preened under his praise. After this morning's meeting with Cora, she was ready to dive in and be happy. She couldn't believe how easy it seemed once you made a decision to do it. A knock on the door and then Daisy entered.

"Hello darlin', here is your lunch," she said, smiling at Gina.

"Thanks, Daisy."

"No worries. Thanks for letting me know he was coming."

Chris turned towards her and smiled. "I didn't realize it was lunchtime."

"I did, sit down. My boards will be up when we finish."

Gina watched him sit down and pull out a sandwich. He unfolded the sandwich exactly the way it had been wrapped.

She looked at her sandwich, it looked like a monster had ripped the wrapping off. When Chris was done unwrapping the sandwich, he laid out a napkin and then cut the sandwich into quarters.

"I think I'm going to be done with my food before you take your first bite."

He looked up and smiled. "I usually can't stay for the whole meal, so I cut it up in small pieces so I can grab a bite and eat on the run and try to preserve the packaging, "he said.

Gina nodded and then touched his hand. "Don't worry if you have to leave, I'll eat it for you. I don't want you to have that responsibility on your shoulders."

Both of them laughed and then began to eat. It would take some getting used to, eating with a guy. She wasn't really accustomed to sharing on a daily basis. She settled in and then thought about all that had happened the last week and remembered what she wanted to tell him.

"Chris, you remember a bit ago you came in, and Michelle was here?"

"Hmm."

"Well, she came in for a reason."

Gina loved watching him dig into his food. She liked this deli and would order again if she could get him to eat up.

"What was the reason?" he asked.

"She needed a loan for eighty thousand or another answer."

"What?"

Gina wouldn't have been able to tell you how, but she knew something was off. When she lifted her head from her sandwich, Chris was looking at her as if she were a mouse, and he was a hawk.

She put down her sandwich. "Don't worry, I didn't give it to her." She thought that statement would diffuse the situation, but he seemed just as intent.

"What did she want the money for?"

"Well, that was a little complicated, but rest assured, I told her no."

"Did she think you had that kind of money to lend?" Chris asked softly. When she heard that crooning tone, she realized this was not going to blow over like she thought.

"Chris, let's talk."

"She knows you don't have that kind of money lying around, that means she wanted to use you to get it from me. I'll have her out by the end of today."

Gina sighed. She looked at her sandwich and realized there would be no happy ending here.

"First, let me say that she knows I don't have it, but her intentions were good."

"Were they? If they were so good, why didn't she go to the bank?"

"Well it's not as clean cut—"

"Gina, she needs to go."

Gina reached out and grabbed both of his hands. "Chris, hear me out." When he didn't speak, she did. "She was trying to give the medical care for the kids and paying the money back but an ex-employee is trying to blackmail her, and that led to another thing, and she needs help."

"What she is, is an opportunist who is trying to use your good nature to—"

"Chris, please. I already told her we wouldn't fire her and that you'd fix this."

He look as if all the air had just been knocked out of him. "You said what?"

"I told her she was foolish. That it was a reckless thing to do and that no amount of good intentions should force us to consider illegal means. In fact, it's because of this situation that—if you look at the third whiteboard up there—you'll see the program I have for those who don't have insurance."

"Gina, we're here to save the community Center, not rescue those who make poor choices."

"Chris, she was desperate and did it from the right place. Doesn't she deserve a second chance?"

"Fine, but I still need to talk to her."

"I knew you'd want to, so she is on your calendar for tomorrow morning."

"Gina?"

"Yes, Chris?"

"Let's look at these plans. It seems I need to understand why we have all of these programs a little better."

Fifteen

"Ah, cola straight from the can," Chris said, opening up the cans and sticking straws in them.

Gina looked at the red cans. "Fresh cola is like fresh, canned tuna. You're depending on science in both situations."

"I could have gotten those brand name drinks, but true romance means nothing distracts you from me."

Gina laughed at his silliness. She would have never thought Chris had a silly side. After this afternoon and her revelation about Michelle, she thought he would stay away, but as soon as the day was over, he waited for her and asked if they could make dinner. She told him right away she had no food in the house, and he suggested they pick up takeout on the way to her home.

She picked up her can, and they toasted. She took a sip from her straw and then closed one eye.

"You're always going so fast," Chris scolded. "Do you have a brain freeze now?"

"Yes, but it's not my fault. It's been a while since I drank cola."

She waited for it to pass, and then took a deep breath. "All the new experiences you are bringing to me."

He smiled. "I know you're feeling enriched by my presence."

"Okay, you've definitely been drinking too much cola."

Chris laughed. They had finished their dinner and had decided to drink the cola on the couch. He had already finished his so she now gave him her can to put on the side.

"I've noticed that this is the second time you've offered food, and we stay at home," Gina teased. "I guess this is what everyone complains about, we don't go out anymore."

"We don't go out because I can't hold you in my arms in public, and this is one of my favorite things to do."

Gina waved his answer off. "You pulled that answer from the man-book of what to say when you're in a bind."

"Ah, but the question is, did it work?"

She leaned back into his arms and relaxed. This was something she didn't do with anyone, and it felt good to do it now.

"Did I tell you that I like your spirit?" he asked.

Again, he knew what to say. All of the things people usually said were too bold.

"My spirit? Is that what they're calling it these days? Usually, people say I'm outspoken."

"I prefer steadfast."

"It could get annoying."

"Only if you are wrong or can't defend your position. I don't think either of those will happen. I mean, you will have to get used to me being right most of the time but—"

"What?"

Chris started laughing again. "Sometimes, Gina, you're too easy to rile."

"Easy?" She pushed up and turned to him. One moment she was about to give him a piece of her mind, and the next, he had pulled her across his lap, and she was looking into his eyes.

"I wouldn't use the word easy to describe you, Gina. I'd use treasure."

He traced the outline of her face until his fingertip came to rest at her chin.

"It's times like these that I realize the simple things I missed. You enrich me, Gina. You give my life a new dimension with your boldness."

Gina had the memory of the last kiss dancing in her head, making her anticipate the kiss she hoped was coming. Her body was tense, and the butterflies in her stomach were churning into a vibration running through her body.

Gina had never felt more alive than she did right now. In his arms, with him looking at her as if she were the most precious person on the planet. The feeling was overwhelming in its intensity but it renewed her at the same time. She reached up and touched his face.

"I'm glad my crazy doesn't bother you. You give me a safe harbor to be me."

He leaned down and pulled her up at the same time. Just when she thought he was going to kiss her, he turned her head to the side and kissed her right below her ear several times. Each kiss as light as a butterfly's wing.

She reached up and slipped her arms under him and traced the bunched muscles of his back. When he reached the crook of her neck, the kisses stopped and he stilled. Not wanting to let go just yet, she held him tighter and then leaned her head towards him. When she did, she could feel his warm breath bathing her skin.

The muscles that were stationary before rose and fell with a noticeable steady beat.

He gave her another kiss and then stood up. She felt as if her world had just been pulled out.

"What's wrong?" she asked.

Chris looked at her and let out a big sigh. "Everything is right, so I'm leaving before I mess it up."

"Chris?" She felt a sense of panic and anger.

"Gina, I need to leave."

She didn't know what to say. Then he reached out and lifted her chin.

"This isn't about you, Gina. I need to do right by you, and if that means I need to leave, then so be it. You are worth doing this the right way."

She laughed hesitantly. "I feel like I've been complimented, yet I'm conflicted. Don't I get a say in all of this?"

"You are an attractive woman, but if I'm going to be your safe harbor, I have to watch out for you even when it goes against what I want to do."

"So, you get to be the knight who makes all the decisions? Oh, whatever, just go. I feel like crazy is upon me."

"It's on us both. For what it's worth, you are not alone in the feeling. Good night Gina."

He didn't kiss her. He didn't linger. He picked up his coat. He made sure she locked the door behind him and then left.

She didn't have to wonder, tonight she'd dream of a man who could walk away for her sake. Chris Griggs had levels to him she'd never thought of.

Sixteen

She had rearranged the meeting site in the hope he'd show some pity. It was a shame Michelle didn't know that when it came to Gina, Chris didn't believe in compromising. He took a seat at the small table in the coffee shop.

"Thank you for meeting me—"

Chris cut her off. "I'm here because Gina asked me. I only have one question for you."

He saw Michelle straighten her back and swallow. "Yes?"

"Can you come up with a reason why I shouldn't just fire you now?"

Michelle looked confused. "Didn't Gina explain that—"

"This isn't about what Gina explained or didn't explain. I've been at the Center for more than a year. If you were having a problem, you should have come to me."

Chris saw the moment that understanding dawned on her.

"You're upset that I went to Gina and not you?"

"Upset doesn't quite capture the feeling I have about this situation."

"I didn't want to go to either one of you! I tried to do everything that I could," Michelle pleaded. "The demands from Larry were just too much, and I had no other options. I didn't know what else to do.

"The only reason I'm even listening to this is because you haven't done anything illegal, just not smart."

"Excuse me? I didn't meet with you today so you could insult me. I admit that I got myself into an issue and I don't know how to fix it."

Chris gave her a long hard look. "That statement probably saved your job."

Michelle hung her head, and her shoulders sagged. "What do you want me to do?"

"I want you to learn how to maneuver in business. I think you are an amazing employee. I think you are passionate and focused on your clients, but you are a horrible business person. Fortunately, I know business. So I'm going to show you how to get yourself out of this mess."

"He's threatening not only me but the clinic as well," Michelle said.

"The first thing I want you to do is to check if that is true. Do you really think if he went to the authorities with what he has, you or the Center would be in trouble?"

Michelle gave him a long look. "He sounded so sure."

"I bet he did."

"If you know the answer already, why do I have to go do this?"

"You have to go do this because this is a part of your job, protecting the Center from opportunists. You need to do this because I believe he targeted you because you were a woman, and an easy target. You can prove him wrong. I can show you how to research and find out if they are real threats or not. If you're willing?"

Michelle nodded. "I'm willing."

"There's a condition that you've got to accept for this to go any further."

"Name it."

"If you have a problem, you need to bring it to me. If Gina gives you a task, that's one thing, you can take it up with her, but when it comes to Center problems, you need to bring those to me, agreed?"

Michelle smiled. "Agreed."

Chris nodded. "Well, let's go over all you know about the problem, and then I'll show you how to handle the issue."

Gina looked at all of the children playing in the yard. They ran around in the playground as their parents received services inside the Center. Today the sun had favored them all and the children were taking advantage of every drop of sunlight. Gina wasn't at a point in her life when she wanted children, but she loved children and believed that they should be cared for.

The toys and general layout of the play yard were Steven's design but it was all funded through Robin's efforts. Gina walked the circumference of the play yard, the little touches could be seen if you looked. The ground was soft with padding and then turf on top of that. The items in the playground came in different sizes. There was something for every child.

"Gina?"

Gina looked around and saw Robin waving at her and making her way over to her.

"I'm glad that you came. I'm sorry I put the meet so last minute on your calendar, but a funder canceled, and I wanted to talk to you as soon as possible."

Gina wasn't so sure Robin had a vacancy, or she wanted to put something together that gave her no time to prepare.

"I made time for now, but I don't have a lot of it to give. I've got a meet with Chris in less than an hour."

Robin nodded. "I understand. Well, I wanted to talk to you about Clara." Robin was shaking her head. "She's acting odd, and there have been some harsh words between her and Tim."

"I just went to a seminar with her and Tim. I didn't think she was under any more stress than anyone else in the group."

Robin nodded. "I respect your opinion but you're wrong. I know Clara and she's acting odd. I've asked her several times and she just says that she can handle it on her own. I know everyone wants to make sure they are efficient, or at least seem efficient, so they don't lose their job, but I'm concerned. On top of that, it seems like it is an open secret that she is seeing Larry Wakefield."

Gina recalled how Michelle spoke of Larry and how Tim had mentioned him as well.

"I've heard the same things when it comes to Larry. I didn't know him, so I'm a little confused about why he's so popular, and it looks like he was let go about six months ago."

"You had to have known Larry. He was a vile man. He was a talented nurse, which seemed to go so counter to his nature, but there it was. When someone had to go, Julia Griggs asked me and I chose him."

"Why did you choose him, Robin?"

Robin looked around the playground and then turned back to Gina. "I think your heart and soul have to be invested in this kind of work. Working in this type of Center can be thankless, and the only reward you'll get is the one you feel when working with the people. Larry wasn't one of those people. When the cut time came, I got rid of the person who didn't work well in groups and thought he should be paid more than anyone else."

"If he was so bad, why is she seeing him then?"

Robin spread her hands out. "I don't know."

Gina heard Robin but she was still unsure. "Okay, we may have a problem but we don't know what it is Larry could be doing. I'm not clear what it is you want me to do about it?"

"It's simple, dear. I've been in this business for a long time. I don't know if you know, but this is my second career. I put my time in as a social worker for the state and retired. Now, I say that to let you know that I'm not here for the money. I'm here because I believe in the cause.

I want you to reach out to Larry and offer him some money to go away. Larry will listen to the fiancée of Chris Griggs."

Gina stopped and looked at Robin.

"Don't look so surprised. I don't like it, but this is how some things are done."

"Have you considered going to Chris?"

Robin walked a little bit around the park, listening to the kids.

"I did consider going to him. Then I thought about it from his point of view. He'd probably clean house and just get rid of Clara and then also be rid of Larry. I didn't want someone who really believed that was the only way to solve the problem, so I'm trying this route."

"I think you're not giving Chris a chance to help."

Robin sighed and gave Gina a wan smile. "Not to state the obvious but you can afford to be a bit more liberal. You're his fiancée. Also, consider before you came, Chris would take care of the books, and Julia did staffing. She's made it very clear she would much rather sell this place and get the money for the land. In short they don't care about what Larry was doing. Larry being a problem is just another justification to get rid of the Center."

"She was working through it then."

Robin shook her head. "Gina, I don't have your luxuries. I think under the right circumstances, Julia Griggs would close the Center in a heartbeat. I've had to argue for us to keep our jobs, but I can't keep that up."

Gina sighed. "That must have been ugly."

"Julia Griggs can bring out the ugly in us all."

Robin looked at the children in the playground. "When I saw how she was so determined to get rid of the Center, I tried to make sure I looked after everyone. When I managed to get funding I used it to boost our position.

Gina looked at Robin and the kids. "It seems obvious this playground is a great feature but I would have thought it would have been one of the first things to go."

Robin turned to Gina. "This playground started without a permit. Steven had set up a mobile playground and volunteered his time every week. Kids started to show up and he kept coming. He was working weekdays then. When the Center was built, he asked to rent this space for those kids.

"A lot of people think that this playground is extra, but to some of the clients, it's the only thing that stops them from falling off the wagon. We have a sliding fee scale, but Steven turns no one away. When I could manage it, I found money to make him a staff member.

"Steven is a computer geek by trade. His taxes from his last job and the pay I give him here are about the same. Never a day does he complain. It's been hard keeping Julia away from Steven. It's one of the reasons I go out and do fundraising. Steven needs the kids and we need Steven.

"I've been around the block a time or two, Gina. I'm not asking for a free ride. I just want to protect the ones that are still here, showing up and present. I'm asking for help to do that."

Robin thought it over. "Clara and Larry?"

"Nothing but my intuition and knowing Clara."

"I'll do my best," Gina said. "If you get an update let me know as well."

"Thanks, Gina. I'm glad you're on our team."

Seventeen

Gina wished Chris was in a good mood because she wasn't going to make it any better for him.

"How did your meet and greet go with Michelle?" she asked.

They were in stop-and-go traffic and Chris looked over at her in the passenger seat.

"Meet and greet? I didn't know there was a new name for supervision before firing. I mean, I've heard of performance improvement plans and even warnings, but meet and greet? That's a new one," Chris said.

"Someone is really grumpy today."

"Grown men don't get grumpy," he muttered.

"Well, how did it go?" Gina pushed.

"It was fine. I spoke with her and now she understands how it works."

"Well, that is good news. I was a little concerned. You know one of the most common mistakes of women is extending themselves too much or taking on too much responsibility. I know she's passionate and wants that to show in her work."

"Yeah."

Gina turned towards him. "So, how did you fix it?"

"Michelle has it."

Gina cocked her head to the side. "You mean you've helped her to a certain point?"

The truck stopped in traffic again and he looked over at her. "I'm giving her a chance to address the issue. We worked out a plan and now she needs to execute it."

"She needs to execute it?"

"She's in this predicament because someone rightly assessed her as being a weak link. If the rumor is true, a man by the name of Larry was blackmailing her into giving up some medications or money."

"She said she had to for the Center and for herself."

"Larry told her that but she needs to check it out. In truth, he couldn't tell on her without getting in trouble himself. If he says she's selling medications, then he has to say he received some. There's a whistleblower rule that protects a person who reports but unless it's a big case, the person doing the reporting can't be the guilty party."

Gina nodded. "That makes sense but the threat must sound really bad when you hear it?"

"It does and when you're alone and targeted, you don't feel like there is anyone you can ask without potentially getting in trouble. Larry has probably made this threat before. If the victim reports it later, the authorities would have no real recourse because Larry would be guilty of lying, and the victim acted out of fear instead of data.

"That's sick to prey on good people." Gina was disgusted at how low people would stoop to steal. "Michelle must have been terrified."

"I suppose she was."

"How did you know it was a fake?"

"I keep up to date on compliance rules. She should too. The fact that she didn't know these rules tells me we need to make sure they are part of the company's annual training."

"Michelle must be happy that all she's worked for isn't at stake."

"I'm sure she will be when she finds out," Chris said.

"Don't you think it's a bit cruel not to tell her?"

Chris sighed. "What I think is Michelle was targeted by a man who isn't as smart as she is or as dedicated to her job. She was targeted because an assumption was made that she wouldn't know what to do and she wouldn't ask for help because she was a woman and scared. I want to give her the tools to never let that happen again."

Gina let his words sink in and while she didn't like the method he was using, she wanted Michelle to be equipped.

"I may not like the way you are helping but what you say is true."

"Are you saying that I'm right over there Gina?" Chris asked with a grin.

"Don't let it go to your head. I know you said you were meeting with some other people about the Center finances?"

"Yes, I did. It's what I thought. The Center is breaking even, but that is common for a nonprofit this size. The issue is someone is moving assets around so that the year-end comes out right, but the three-month trial balances are all over the place."

Gina was disappointed. "So you were right. Someone is causing these problems."

"I'm just trying to narrow down the suspects."

Gina felt Chris reach over and pat her leg. "I'm sorry I don't have the answers you want but it will be over soon."

Gina remembered Robin and her problem and what she wanted to talk to Chris about on the car ride.

"Cheer up Gina, let's talk about a happier topic."

"Like?"

"Like us, of course."

At the mention of "us", she was transported back to their last kiss. Who knew one word could render such images? Gina swallowed. "It's good that you brought it up because I want to talk about that as well."

"What did you want to talk about? Are you having doubts about—"

"Oh no, Chris, it's nothing like that. I was thinking that maybe it was time that we told everyone that we're not engaged."

"Really," he said gently.

Gina turned a confused gaze towards Chris. "What's wrong?"

When the car stopped, he looked at her with an annoyed look. "Well, I don't know what could be right when the woman I thought I was in a relationship with says we shouldn't be engaged anymore?"

"You're misunderstanding. You see I think a lot of people don't come to you with problems because they don't really know you. Since I'm posing as your fiancée, they don't need to and they come to me."

"So, is this because I was upset with Michelle for coming to you?"

"No, but maybe yes. I don't want to say that. What I want to say is it's awkward. So if we remove this barrier then—"

"I've got a better idea. How about we explain nothing and you become my fiancée?"

Gina stopped, and then anger spurred her into action. "Are you serious?"

"Yes I—"

"Are you seriously going to ask me to be your fiancée in a car? Where you can't even look me in the eye for more than two minutes?"

"Not a problem."

Chris put on his hazard lights and pulled to the curb. Gina watched him do it and her mouth hung ajar. When they were slanted on the side of the road, she looked at him as if he were crazy.

"Gina, would you like to be my fiancée?"

She looked around him and out the window. Every so often, a car honked at them as they went around the truck.

"What are you doing?"

"I'm asking you to be with me forever. I know we're on the slow path but I'm sure about what I'm doing here."

She looked at him and in that moment it became too real. She could feel her vision getting blurred and the heat building in her chest. "Maybe you need some more time to think about—"

"To think about forever with you? Clearly I can see this is not what you were expecting so let's meet in the middle."

"We're negotiating?" she asked incredulously.

"Will you be my fiancée Gina? I'm not asking for anything beyond that. I just want to know if you trust me enough for that?"

"What if getting married makes it all go south?" she whispered.

He lifted her chin. "I've got you. We'll work it out."

Before she could answer, a tap on the window had them both turning to see a policeman standing outside of the truck. Chris rolled down the window.

"Officer?"

"You having car problems?" The office was an older man and his eyes were taking in everything as he spoke. "Ma'am, are you alright?"

Gina nodded.

Chris cleared his throat.

"I'm sorry officer I had to pull over to the side of the road to ask her if she'd be my fiancée."

The officer looked over at Gina. She nodded. "He did officer."

The officer looked at the truck and then at Chris.

"What's wrong with a restaurant or a nice hall? Did you answer? Because you can't stay here on the side like this. Your tail is hanging out in the road."

Gina looked at Chris. "So Gina, the officer wants to know what your answer is."

Gina grinned. "The officer wants to know? Let me get out and let him know—"

"I want to know, as well."

Gina looked at the officer. "I said yes. He'll be moving now."

The officer looked at Gina and then at Chris. "You've got your hands full, best of luck to you both."

Eighteen

She didn't feel any different today. She should feel something after making the engagement real. Shouldn't she? As she walked into the office, Daisy gave her a nod.

"Gina, I'm giving you a heads-up Mama. Julia Griggs has an appointment with her brother. The word is she wants to get some decisions on what is going on."

"Is she here yet?"

"No, but soon Mama."

"Can you call Chris and ask him to meet me in my office."

"I got ya."

Gina walked to her office and thought about what they should say to Julia. She had just put her coat down and was about to take her seat when she heard the knock on the door.

"Come in," she called out.

The door opened, and it was like watching a horror movie. Would it be Chris alone, or would it be Chris and Julia who came in together? When it was just him, she gave him a smile and let go of the breath she was holding. He didn't stop. He walked up to her and kissed her neck. How did he do that so casually?

"You okay, Gina?"

She waved him off, trying fan herself off at the same time. "I'm good. I heard that your sister is coming."

"You heard correctly. She's coming in about thirty minutes."

"Well, what are you going to say?"

He leaned against the door and had a confused look on his face. "What do you mean?"

"What I mean is you can't tell her that there is foul play at the Center."

"I can't?"

"No! Until we know who it is and how to address it, we don't want to put any dampers on the Center. We also don't want to talk about Michelle. Like you said, she's handling it, so that's almost a non-issue."

"So, I'm curious Gina. What would you like me to tell my sister when she arrives?"

"I expect you to tell her you have it all under control and that it's going according to plan."

"Really?"

"Chris!"

"I don't know this may set a bad precedent with us in our relationship. At the core of our relationship, we're friends, and the thing I've learned about friends is that they need to be honest and transparent. I want to make sure I practice those attributes so I can give them to my fiancée."

Gina looked at him in disbelief. "I can't believe you are feeding me this line."

"Now, I am not unsympathetic to your cause. As a result, I want to help you, but this kind of thing could weigh heavily on me and—"

"What do you want, Chris?"

Chris placed his hand on his chest in mock horror. "Want something? I wouldn't think of asking, but if you were offering, of course, I would be interested in hearing what you would put on the table for this timely task."

"I'm asking again, what do you want?"

Chris brushed the back of his hand over her cheek. "I want the most expensive thing you have."

Gina had to concentrate not to follow his hand as it warmed her cheek. She could feel the tendrils of desire run through her body until it pooled in her stomach and made her stand up straighter.

"I give up, what is it?"

She watched his head lean closer to her, until she could feel his breath against her ear. "Time, Gina. I want time with you, whenever I choose. No warning."

Gina swayed towards him when she heard the request. Her head fell forward, and she could feel his breath go down the column of her throat. Her eyes closed, and she floated in the warm space between thinking about his kisses and grabbing hold of his shoulders to offer herself up for kisses.

When her forehead brushed against his neck she cleared her throat and pulled herself back to the present. Stepping away, she looked at him and gave him what she hoped was her best look of disapproval.

"Done. I don't know why you'd ask for anything since we've upgraded our relationship."

Chris smiled. "I like that. Upgraded our relationship."

"Look I'll pick a place and let you—"

"No, Gina, that's not what I said."

She looked at him as if he had lost his mind. "Well, when did you want to go out?"

Chris backed away with a smile. "That's the whole point. I'll let you know when I want to cash in my time. That's the price, Gina."

Gina hesitated. "I hear you, but I'm not sure why it's being presented this way. I feel like I'm walking into a trap."

Chris opened the door. "I'm hurt you think I'd trap you, but I understand how you might feel that way. I would stay and help you move past this, but I have to go and talk to my sister."

He walked out the door, and Gina knew she had just signed up for more than she guessed, but she knew he was good to his word, and he'd handle his sister and the Center.

She had been waiting on pins and needles for Chris to come into the office after his sister left. Instead, Chris had to go into one meeting after another and what Gina thought would be a few minutes wound up being hours. When her phone rang, she thought it was Chris and grabbed it.

"Yes?"

"Hello, Mama, it's Daisy. I have Michelle on the phone. She wanted to speak to Chris, but he's still on a business call for another ten minutes. Can you talk to her?"

"Of course."

"Hello Michelle, it's me, Gina."

"Oh, Hi, Gina. I thought Chris was going to pick up."

"No worries. He's on the other line. Can I help you?"

"No, I just wanted to thank Chris. I was really scared when I met with him. When I thought I was going to lose my job, it really helped me focus?"

"Thought you were going to lose your job?"

"Well, he didn't say it that way, but you know Chris. He asked me why he shouldn't fire me on the spot. I know I needed that wake-up talk, and I wanted to tell him I'm making progress, and he was right about everything."

"I'll make sure to tell him."

"Thanks, Gina."

When Gina hung up the phone she took a deep breath. She knew there must be some misunderstanding. Certainly Chris hadn't threatened Michelle. Call or no, this was too important. She got up and went to his office. She opened the door and found him still talking on the phone, but when he saw Gina, he ended the call and stood up.

As he came arms open to Gina, she held up her hand.

"I have to ask you a question."

"Shoot."

"Did you threaten Michelle with firing her."

"No, I wasn't threatening her. I had every intention of firing her if she needed to be fired."

"What?"

"Yes, Gina. I would have fired her if it were in her best interest."

"Okay, I'm listening."

Chris sat down and looked at her. "Gina, you are a strong woman."

"Yes," she said, trying to be open-minded about where this might be going.

"If Michelle wants to stay at the Center, she has to be strong enough to fend off the predators who will come. That means I have to make sure she understands what is at stake and what her responsibility is."

"Chris, I agree, but I sent you to her to help her not to make her feel worse," Gina said defensively.

"I did what I thought would be best for her as well."

Gina took a breath and looked at him. "It took me by surprise because I didn't expect you to handle it that way."

Chris looked at her and cocked his head to the side. "I'll run it by you next time, but in the end, if you ask me to help someone, I can only help them in the way I know how. Agreed?"

"Agreed."

"Well, I think that qualifies as our first real argument."

Gina stared at him, incredulously. "Really? You're counting that as an argument?"

"It's all in the eye of the beholder, so yes."

"Well, congratulations. We can put this in our book of firsts," Gina said.

"I've got a better idea."

Nineteen

"I want my time now," Chris announced.

Gina looked at him as if he had lost his mind. She shrugged her shoulders and then looked over hers.

"Is this a joke? It's the middle of the day?"

Chris looked at his watch and nodded. "This time works great for me." He picked up his phone on the desk and dialed Daisy.

"Yes, Mr. Griggs."

"Daisy, I'm in a meeting with Gina, and I can't be disturbed for the next hour, okay?"

They both heard Daisy twittering like a schoolgirl on the other end. "Of course, Mr. Griggs."

"You so know what she thinks is going on in here," Gina admonished.

Chris shrugged, "Does it matter?"

"Okay, we're in here for an hour, and this is your time. What do you want to do?"

Chris went behind his desk and brought out a brown wicker basket. It had a closed top on it, and it aroused her curiosity.

"What's inside?" she asked, moving closer. Chris patted the flat wicker basket and then looked at Gina.

"I know you can't tell now, but my sister is the most compassionate and caring person I know. She's just hurt and having some issues, but all in all, she is the one who taught me about giving back and not taking anything for granted. We had parents, but my mom spent a lot of time trying to get my dad in line, and that left me with Julia. So, Julia said I needed to control my temper and give back. I want to share that with you."

Chris opened the basket and pulled out two balls of yarn and two sets of knitting needles.

"You're joking right?"

Chris smiled. "Nope, I'm not."

"Really Chris? I thought we were going to do something—"

Chris gave her a wan smile. "You wanted to do something that was fun. You're probably right."

Gina watched Chris as he placed the yarn back into the basket and saw him deflate a bit as he did so.

"Okay, okay, I'll try it but no guarantees. Okay?"

Chris nodded. "Okay, let's get started."

Twenty minutes later, after going over the basics, Chris smiled at Gina and said, "Okay, let's pick a scarf pattern."

Gina looked in the basket and found several patterns. She picked the one with a Celtic knot and twists that ran on the side. She handed it to Chris and smiled.

"Gina, this is supposed to be relaxing for us both. Are you sure you want to do this one first?"

"Yes, I think we should do the hardest stuff first."

Chris smiled and agreed. "Okay, I need you to remember, knits in the front and purls in the back."

Gina smiled and nodded.

"Okay, let's cast on 20 chain stitches."

For the next thirty minutes, Chris gave Gina instructions so she could knit the first five lines of the scarf. He didn't do it for her, but he guided her through it.

Gina looked at the small square and held it up for Chris to see. "Look! If we can do this together and you don't want to kill me for taking out the chains and starting over four times, we can fix anything. Or we can elect you for sainthood."

Chris laughed as he collected the items.

"My sister told me I was impatient and that more than once she wanted to just stop teaching me to knit. I can't remember when I was that bad, but she claims it was so." He said with a shrug, and they both laughed.

Gina's curiosity got the better of her as they were packing up. "Chris, why this?"

He paused and looked at Gina intently. "I think tradition is important, and it's something I'd like to share with you. I know you said you didn't have a stable home life growing up. I was hoping that this could be a new tradition for us both. Something old and something new."

These were the moments that Chris showed her a part of himself that she would treasure always. She didn't think she'd ever be any good at knitting, but she wanted to keep trying for Chris.

Cora had told her she didn't get to choose who her heart would want, but that it would definitely be worth the ride.

Someone knocked on the door, and they both looked up. Daisy's voice came through loud and clear.

"If you are going to be doing this every day, you're going to have to keep your voices down. People said they heard you two laughing and Gina saying 'Stop I can do it,' and Chris in their moaning, 'No not again let's just finish it.'"

They stared at one another for a second before they both burst out laughing. Yeah, it didn't get any better than this, Gina thought as she held her belly and laughed.

The next morning Gina was summoned by her future sister-in-law to a country club so they could get acquainted. Gina worried that no good would come from it and suspected that this meeting had more to do with Chris' vague answers of yesterday.

Gina found herself sitting at a side table in a very nice restaurant. Julia Greggs had on a wraparound grey dress that somehow looked dignified on her slim frame. She was drinking tea and Gina was waiting for coffee. It had started out well, Julia had a smile on her face and she looked pleasant enough.

Then pleasantries had ended. Julia was now giving all types of signals that she was not a happy woman, and she wanted answers. Her grey and white, one-inch heels were tapping on the ground in a rhythm that sounded more and more like a ticking clock. She sighed so often that it made Gina think she was a coal fed train about to take off. All of that though was secondary to the way she crossed and uncrossed her legs as if she weren't sure what to do with them.

"I'll get right to the point, Gina. I spoke to my brother yesterday. I expected him to give me an update on the Center, but instead, he fed me a line about how the two of you had it all under control."

Gina kept her face straight and nodded. Again, she would have to work with Chris on how he did things she asked. The man was so literal.

"I can understand why he'd say that. We've been working on it, and like Chris says, I think we've got it almost ironed out."

"I don't think you understand my concern. I know you are his fiancée and that sharing is important, but I have to ask you a question. Do you really think that you are qualified to assist him in this business? I understand you are a project manager, but this is a business Chris and I have cultivated. To have him give such sparse details is a potential danger to all we've built."

Gina was startled by the attack and the steel in her voice when she spoke of the threat Chris' lack of disclosure could be causing.

"I can't speak to the potential danger, but I will say that I trust Chris. If he didn't give you all the details, I'll accept responsibility for that. However, I'm confident that Chris would never do anything to endanger the company you two built. He believes in having all the information before making any assessments, he's very thorough that way."

"We all are," Julia said. "We need to be of one accord. If you have a pet project you want to do, that's fine. However, when it comes to Chymera, this is not a playground for the current love of his life."

Gina wanted to make sure her anger didn't get the better of her tongue. "I'm not here to push my way into your family business, however, this Center is something Chris asked me to do with him. If there is an issue or some discussion on my involvement, then please take it up with Chris."

She didn't stay and drink the coffee as it arrived. Instead, she found the exit, got a cab, and then went back to her place. She called Daisy and told her she wouldn't be in for the day, in case anyone was looking for her.

Twenty

"I can't believe how she spoke to me," Gina said as she dished up another chopstick full of lo mein. "She treated me like I was a child and didn't know what I was doing," Gina ranted.

Chris was sitting at the table in Gina's house. He had picked up some chocolates and Danishes. It was just the two of them on the couch.

"I'll talk to her, and I want to thank you for not losing your cool with her," he said. Chris knew there was a reckoning coming between him and Julia, and he wasn't looking forward to it. "There's no excuse for it, and I'll have to address it."

"It was just condescending. She made it seem like you were so infatuated with your new fiancée that you'd let me do something that would put your company at risk."

"Well, I am infatuated, but I wouldn't put the company at risk. I will carefully consider everything you ask me for."

Gina stopped ranting and gave him a silly grin. "Oh, you just keep those little zingers in your pocket, don't you?"

"I do my best, madam," Chris said, bowing theatrically.

"There's so much going on, and we're so close to getting the Center right, I wish she would just go on vacation and leave us alone until the kinks are all worked out."

"I can't give you that," Chris said solemnly.

Gina stopped and let out a big sigh. "All that being said, I did feel bad for her. She seems like she's trying to hold it together. She looked off at the meeting at the Center, and she seemed to have a quiet kind of rage when she spoke to me."

Chris smiled. "It's odd you want her gone, but not hurt. You want her to feel better, but you don't want her in on everything."

Gina smiled. "I know it sounds crazy, ugh! I need to clear my head. Let's talk about something else. How about we talk about you?"

"I think that subject has been beaten to death," Chris said.

"Come on, tell me how it's been going with you getting up to speed and talking with the rest of the employees in the city?"

"I'm making progress. I've read your project plans. I think that everything is moving along."

Gina tilted her head as he spoke. "I feel like you're giving me lip service."

"There are still some inconsistencies I'm tracking down. I've got a friend who is discrete and can investigate these things better than I could."

"I had hoped we were past these suspicions."

Chris shook his head. "If anything, I think we've confirmed that there is a case of someone doing something. I may not be able to say if it's malicious or not, but I can tell you there is a pattern."

"How's being engaged?" she asked playfully.

"Well, even though she can't knit. She shows great potential. Also, it's like everyone knows I'm engaged, and I look more attractive."

"You know the saying: everyone wants what they can't have. Is it more real to you now? Do you regret—"

Chris cut her off. "I don't regret it at all. I know I should have done this earlier. I ignore the sly-eyed invitations. I have what I want already."

"This was all so sudden. Is there no one who made you question making our engagement real?"

He moved the food and pillows that were between them to the coffee table. He looked her in the eye. "If I looked at a woman, it was always in a sisterly way." He cradled her hand and ran his thumbs over her skin. "I have to deal with my sister. I always knew I'd have to deal with her. It was part of what I didn't want to expose you to. I'm not just Chris Griggs. When you said yes to me, you said yes to being in Chymera, and you said yes to adopting Julia in all of her thorniness."

"I don't have a problem with that. I'm not just a pretty face, you know."

Chris gave her a smile, and it made her catch her breath and focus on the matter at hand. Not his hands that were rubbing circles on hers but the topic they were discussing.

He let her hand go and went to get his jacket. He had laid it and a medium box on the other side of the couch. "We're engaged, and I've been remiss in my duty. I will start making it up to you right away, but I wanted to start with something that would mean something to just us two."

He picked up the box and gave it to her.

"You didn't have to. I don't—"

He placed a fingertip on her lips. "The custom goes that when a woman gets engaged, she gets gifts from the man and his family because *she* is a gift. To honor that custom, I give you this. One gift of many."

Gina took the box and opened it up. Inside was a knitted Celtic scarf. She pulled it up, loving that it was the pink she had chosen to work with.

"You shouldn't have. You must not have slept in order to do this."

"I slept, and I confess I had to start over once."

She looked at him and laughed before throwing herself into his arms.

He held her tightly. "Will you stay in my arms for a moment?"

Gina couldn't speak, so she nodded her head.

Warmth spread through her until she thought she was vibrating. Chris' hands never moved from her back, but they pulled her closer, and she could feel his breath in her hair. He pulled back and looked into her face.

"Never forget you are more precious to me than anything, you are the gift I was afraid to accept."

He stepped away, and she felt bereft without him. She pulled the scarf closer to her chest and watched him gather his coat.

"You're leaving?" she asked.

"I am."

"This seems to be a trend. You come over. You bring food. You leave me with cleanup," she said in a teasing voice.

"That's the story today. I'm working on changing the ending. Good night, Gina."

She had no comeback for that, and when the door closed, it was as if she came out of a slumber.

Twenty-one

Gina was thinking about last night when she picked up her phone.

"Gina?" said a voice with a slight hitch in it, and just like that, her whole mood was destroyed.

"Yes?"

"It's me, Clara. Can we talk?"

"Of course." Gina got a pen and paper to write down the address she would meet Clara at. Gina understood that subtext. Clara wasn't sure if Chris was here. She'd meet her in a coffee shop.

Gina wasn't thrilled to be going, but it did look like Chris' pep speech was making the rounds and inspiring the troops. As she was leaving the building, she stopped by Daisy.

"Is Chris in, Daisy?"

"No, he's not in the building. He's booked with meeting most of the day. Do you want to leave a message?"

"No, it's okay I don't know anything yet. See you later."

Gina walked into the bright coffee shop and had to take a moment to appreciate the interior. She would never have found the place without instructions from Clara. On the outside, it looked like a dingy hole in the wall, but inside the walls were pastel, and the smell of coffee floated in the central ac store.

She spotted Clara sipping coffee at a high table. The waitress, who was cleaning up near Clara's chair, nodded to Clara, making Gina think they might have known each other. That would mean that the coffee house was probably a regular spot for Clara.

"Thank you for coming, Gina."

"I figured it had to be important for you to call me," Gina replied.

Clara flinched and then took a breath. "I have a problem named Larry Wakefield."

"That man seems to get around," Gina said. "So, what is it that he has on you?"

Clara's jaw tightened. "Equipment. I give out flip phones to my clients."

"Okay?"

"I give them to anyone who can show they are looking for a job. They have all given them back, with the exception of maybe one or two, and I've replaced those."

"What's the problem?" Gina asked.

"I have phones as part of my program. It's not a reimbursable portion. The phones are never part of a bill, so it's just a loss."

"So, let me guess, you are working with Larry on this?"

Clara's stricken expression was enough answer for Gina.

"So how did Larry find out?"

"I don't know, but he does know. He was going to say I was renting out phones."

"You're not so what's the issue?" Gina asked.

"Behavioral health is a small field. Sometimes it doesn't matter if you're guilty are not. People will judge you and the agency you worked with and find you guilty no matter what."

"I suppose he wants money as well?" Gina said.

Clara nodded. "I spoke to Michelle, and she said I have to take a stand. I think when I tell him no, he's going to tell everyone anyway. I was hoping I could meet with you to help you prepare. I thought maybe you could fire me and then put the story out first. Beat him to the punch."

Gina looked at Clara, sitting on the high chair with her head held high. Her hands were tightly clasped around her clutch purse as she spoke of how she would end the career she loved. Then Robin's words came back to Gina. "The people at the Center were the believers."

"So, if you don't give him money, what does he want?"

"He wants me to give him the inventory and order better quality items."

"So, there are some challenges here. Chris knows inventory is missing, and he's tracking it now."

Then all the fight went out of Clara.

"I've been trying to do my best and make it right. I just—"

Gina had heard enough. It was time to put a stop to this.

"We are going to make a stand and get rid of Larry Wakefield. Where is Larry these days?" Gina asked.

"He opened up a nurse on-call company."

"Well then, let's go pay him a visit."

With his address in hand, Gina decided a surprise visit was the way to go. She'd already sent a text to Chris that she wanted to bring him up to speed on an issue. Now she had to make sure Larry didn't think it was open season on the New Hope Center employees.

It didn't take long to find the address for Larry's business of on-call nurses. His signs were tacky and huge, and he'd named the company Larry's Angels. Clara stood beside her as they looked on the building directory for the floor.

"Gina, what are you going to do?"

"I'm going to explain to him that Chris is in charge of things and that when he tries to blackmail the employees at New Hope, he's really blackmailing Chris," Gina explained.

"Chris, as in Chris Griggs?" Clara looked paler than she had earlier. "Don't you think you should discuss this with Chris first?"

"No, I don't need to discuss it because he believes in empowering women. And hopefully, it won't even become a conversation. If all goes well, this will be the first and last time we need to be here."

Clara walked with Gina into the elevator and crossed her arms over her chest. "I'm not feeling as optimistic as you are. We can turn back and try to regroup with Michelle and—"

The doors opened. "Too late, let's get this done."

Gina walked up to the desk and smiled at the young lady sitting behind it. "Hello, we'd like to see Mr. Wakefield."

"Yes, I'm sure you would, as would a lot of people, but that's not possible. He's booked."

"I think you should look again because if I leave this office the next time you see my name, it will be on a subpoena to Mr. Wakefield," Gina responded with a smile.

The young lady picked up the phone and murmured into it. When she hung up, they heard a buzz, and they were let into Larry's office.

When Gina walked into the office, she could see how the women were taken in. Larry Wakefield was an attractive man in an expensive suit who looked like he had just walked off the pages of an Armani ad.

"Ladies, to what do I owe the pleasure?"

Gina stepped forward. "I actually came here to ask you to stop blackmailing my employees."

Larry looked at Gina and then clapped as if he were giving a standing ovation. "I have to say that is the most entertaining thing I've heard all day." He looked at Clara, who seemed to be trying to hide behind Gina. "I hope you have what's mine Clara."

Clara stood with a wobbly voice. "I don't have anything that's yours."

"Really, Clara, I don't want to hear your excuses. I want money or merchandise."

Gina stopped Clara from replying.

"Mr. Wakefield, I'm sorry, you didn't understand. I'm not suggesting, I'm telling you, this is over."

"I don't know who you think you are, but this goes on as long as I say it will. Clara will run to Robin, and she will find a way and give me what I want. Julia Griggs can't stand the Center and it's only a matter of time before she sells it. I want my share since I was fired."

"I'm sorry to inform you that the Center has moved from Julia Griggs' hands to Chris Griggs' hands. He will not tolerate this type of action on his employees."

"None of the Griggs care enough to get involved."

"That might have been, but things have changed."

"I'm sorry, I didn't get your name? I would like to know who to send the flowers to when I win."

Gina turned and smiled at him. "I'm Gina, Mr. Griggs fiancée. You'll be hearing my name again but not for the reasons you were thinking."

Clara and Gina walked out of Larry's office. Clara was going on and on about how it went so poorly and what were they going to do? Gina told her to calm down, and she'd call her tomorrow. Once she had Clara in a car and on her way home, she went to the office and sat at her desk. What she really needed now was a piece of chocolate to make it through the night.

Twenty-two

Gina hoped that all the decorations had put Chris into a good mood. The Center was decorated in greens and reds. All around, there were bowls with balloons. Some of the balloons were regular balloons and some had water in them. She walked into his office, and there he was, pouring over reports.

"Hey, I've got great news!"

"I could use some," Chris said. "Let's hear yours."

"Well, it's backhanded good news, but it solves a problem, and that is what is most important. Now, that being said, I want you to be patient and listen to everything first."

Chris leaned forward on his desk and gave Gina a skeptical look. "What have you done?"

"Well, I solved the inventory issue."

"We must finally be in sync because I was about to talk about that too."

Gina gave it three seconds of thought before she decided to go big. "I know who it is!"

"I do too Clara."

"Wow, you already know the story about Clara?"

"The story about Clara the phone thief. I kept telling you that things weren't just happening, and now I have the proof."

"Of course, you were right, Chris," Gina said. "The thing is there were extenuating circumstances, and it will be clear to you once you—"

"Clear to me?" Chris said in a low tone. He looked at Gina as she stepped closer to his desk, and she could tell when it came to him. "You have another person you want to save, Gina?"

"It's not a matter of saving a person. It's a matter of doing the right thing."

"The right thing? The right thing was not to have the company buy hardware it didn't need."

"I hear you Chris but when you look at all the facts—"

"Good, I'm glad you bring in that word, facts. That's what we need to look at here. I wanted to make a difference, but I can't ignore basic business rules to do it."

"Chris, this Center is a needed resource, and all of the people who work here make that happen."

"We can't make that happen with a thief—"

"Thief, Chris, really?"

"I have proof. She was buying without a secondary authorization."

"Does it matter that she was blackmailed into it? Or do we not care about the people and their work, just what shows up on the bottom line?"

"How can this happen to me?" Chris moaned. He knew where this was going.

"Chris, if I hadn't verified it myself, I wouldn't be able to say it."

"Verified it? How did you do that? What documents were enough?" Chris asked.

"I didn't rely on any documents. I made sure I heard it directly from all parties."

"You see, that's the problem if you've already heard it that means that they already went to you to save them." Chris ran his hands through his hair and then let out a long breath. "Okay, Gina, tell me what the story was this time."

"She was giving out phones as loaners, and he was perverting it."

"He?"

"Larry Wakefield. He thinks that he was unjustly let go, and he wants to get what he thinks is his fair share of lost income."

"This is what Clara said?"

Gina nodded. "Yes, she did tell me, but I didn't take her at her word. I went to see Larry, and he—without prompting from he—corroborated the story."

Gina said the last statement as a matter of fact, and then the bravado began to drain out of her when Chris looked at her for a moment and became very quiet.

"Hold on. It's just coming to me what you're saying and what it means."

Gina thought about all the festivities in the Center. She had originally thought it would be great because maybe Chris would be in a great mood, but now she was thinking it would be great so no one would hear him yelling. Chris went back to his seat and then folded his hands together and took deep breaths. Gina had never seen so many emotions cross his face all at once.

"So let me get this straight Gina. You went to see Larry by yourself?"

"No, I wouldn't do that! I took Clara with me."

He held his head in his hands and wouldn't even look at her. Instead, she heard his murmurings.

He finally looked up at her, and Gina took a step back when she saw the rage on his face.

"Chris?"

"What were you hoping to do by going? Did he know you were my fiancée?"

"Yes, I told him."

"You told him. Of course, you told him. Why did I think anything else?" he said as he threw his hands up in the air.

Gina didn't like the way the conversation was going, and she didn't like the way Chris was acting.

"What's your problem, Griggs? I went to see a person, and I had to take care of some things for our business."

"No, Gina! I need you to understand that you went somewhere today and told them you were a Griggs. It means that if he would have taken you hostage or decided to do something to you it would have put all of Chymera at risk."

She looked at him, and the force of what she had done hit her. She had been reckless and had thought about nothing but taking care of Clara. Of course, she knew who Griggs was, but she hadn't thought about the idea that anyone would want to take her to get to Chris. She just hadn't attributed that value to herself in any way, form, or fashion. Like a battering ram, Julia's words came back to her about how she could be a danger to Chymera.

"I didn't think about it, Chris," she whispered.

Chris sat back in his chair. "Let's get it all out. Why did you go see him, for the proof?"

Gina shook her head. The conversation where she was going to explain why she had to defend Clara now seemed so silly compared to what could have happened.

"I wanted to tell him to stop, and if he didn't, I told him you'd take care of him because you were running the Center now, not Julia."

Chris smiled. "Well, let it never be said that you don't have the brazenness needed to play poker with the big boys."

Gina gave a wan smile. "It seemed like the only thing he would fear. I thought about what you were saying before and I thought the reason Larry was targeting the staff was because they appeared to be women. It didn't really matter, though. He just about laughed at me and thought you wouldn't even be bothered with this."

"Did he? I'll correct that for him later."

Gina gave him a smile and nodded. "I knew we'd be able to take care of this."

"It's a funny thing how you say *we're* going to take care of things all the time, but you go off and do something, and then I have to finish it. I don't mind the finish, Gina, but you just going off has scared years off my life."

She watched and waited for the explosion, but it didn't come.

"So, you're not mad?"

"Mad doesn't even begin to address how I feel. I think the best thing I can do is go take care of some other things, so I don't say anything I'll regret about how foolish I think your actions were yesterday."

Every word Chris said was like a verbal slap, and Gina looked at him, not believing this was the way he was going to leave it.

"Chris?"

Chris held up his hand. "Gina, just give me a little bit to adjust to everything. I need to think this over, and you do too. This will be a part of your new life. You will have to be mindful that you are part of a big company and going off to rescue our employees is something we'd be doing together. No more lone-soldier for you, Gina. Griggs don't do that. There's too much at stake. You need to decide if you can abide by that. It's about your safety, Gina."

Twenty-three

To say things had been strained would have been an understatement. Chris missed Gina, and she seemed to have shrunk into a shell of business he couldn't penetrate. He thought he'd try something generic and work his way into groveling.

When he'd invited her to dinner and she accepted, he felt like a kid at Christmas. Chris wanted to leave nothing to chance, so he picked a restaurant that knew him. Of course, the night he decided to go everyone he knew was on vacation or ill. When tyhe went to the restaurant, they couldn't seat him in his usual seat. Then someone recognized his name and asked for a few moments to get him equal accommodations.

A young waiter came over, and before he could say anything a frustrated Chris looked at the boy and shook his head. "Just the menus."

"Of course, Mr. Griggs." The young waiter had on a bright smile and tried to quickly scurry away from the table. Gina held out her hand, and the waiter seemed to tremble.

"Did you say your name was Ron?"

The waiter looked at his chest and then nodded. "Yes, ma'am."

"Thank you, Ron."

The waiter nodded at Gina and then ran off.

"Chris, there's no reason to be scary. He's young."

"Well, we're not friends, and he doesn't know us," Chris said, glaring at the waiter's back.

"Is this another one of those things that comes with being a Griggs?" Gina murmured softly.

Chris sighed and picked up the menu. This night was not starting out on the right foot. He thought about all the things he wanted to say to her, and it suddenly became clear he should have opted for Chinese food at her place. Chris was loath to say it, but he was scared to hear the answers to the questions that needed to be asked.

After the Clara event and their talk, he needed to know if she was still okay with becoming a Griggs. If she could see herself living with him. After their talk three days ago, she'd become quiet and stayed in her office. He wanted to ask her if she would stay with him.

Tonight she was dressed in a blue wrap dress. It crisscrossed over her chest and accentuated her waist. The dress played peek-a-boo with her shape. Never clinging to one place or another and only giving a glimpse to the curves beneath it.

He had made the decision to leave when he looked up and saw the general manager coming towards him. Okay, so every person he knew wasn't on vacation. He knew the skittish waiter probably ran back to the manager in the back, and now they had decided he needed special attention.

"Hello Mr. Griggs."

"Hello Carstairs," Chris said pleasantly.

"Is everything okay, Mr. Griggs?"

"It's fine," Chris said tightly. He knew he was making Carstairs uneasy, but he just wanted some peace and quiet so he could work out this issue with Gina. Just when he was about to tell Carstairs they had to go, he felt her hand on his.

"Hello, Mr. Carstairs. I'm Gina. Chris wanted to bring me here because he said the service was impeccable, I'm so glad to meet you."

Mr. Carstairs bowed and smiled, thanking Chris and flashing a smile at Gina. When Chris saw how happy she had made Carstairs, he realized that's what Gina did. She put others before herswlf and made sure everyone was safe. She'd done it with Clara and Michelle, and she seemed to do it in everything she did.

He suddenly came to the realization that Gina wasn't going to have to adjust to being a Griggs. The Griggs would have to find a way to adjust to Gina. Now that he had thought about it, he couldn't imagine it happening any other way. Changing Gina wasn't an option. The Griggs would live up to the name of the company and change with her. With his epiphany realized, Chris was ready to go.

"Chris, what's wrong? I think you've been cranky for the last couple of days. Did you find something else in the books?"

"No."

"Okay, then is it Larry? I was hesitant to bring it up, considering all the hoopla I caused going to see him. Is he going to be a problem?"

"No, I've dealt with Larry's before he won't be a problem. You know, I'm no good at waiting. I think we should have a talk Gina." He looked up and around the restaurant. This couldn't be a coincidence. He wouldn't believe it even if they told him it was. They were a motley crew so out of place that the maître d looked as though they would stop them, and then they spoke to one another, and the maître d pointed towards him. Well, that was it. Whatever plans he had on leaving were now officially gone. With that, he picked up his napkin and placed it on the table. "Well, there goes the evening."

"What's wrong now?" Gina asked. Gina looked over her shoulder. "Look, it's Robin and Steven."

"Oh yeah, it just keeps getting better," Chris muttered. "I don't know why I thought I had to do this away from everyone." He settled down and waited for them to come to the table.

Robin was dressed in black pants, a white blouse and a black vest. Steven had on clothing that looked like dark jeans and a blue jean top. Steven pulled out a chair for Robin, and they sat down.

"Daisy said you'd be here tonight," Steven said.

"Glad to know that we have communal schedules," Chris quipped. "I suppose it's my penalty for not following my gut."

"Chris, really," Gina said under her breath.

Gina turned to Robin and Steven and smiled. "It's good to see you both. Was there something you wanted with Chris?"

Steven looked at Chris and shook his head. "No, I came here for you, Gina."

"Me?" Gina asked.

"Yes, Clara told me how you went to Larry's office when she was scared, and I wanted to thank you."

Robin tapped the tabletop and Chris looked to see what she was doing.

"It turns out I'm here for you, Griggs," she said with a smile.

"Michelle explained how you helped her to fix the mess she was in, but more importantly, she explained how you were able to help her feel empowered to solve her own issues."

Chris cleared his throat. "She's a smart woman."

"She is a smart woman, but she needed some pointers on what to do. We are all grateful that you addressed Larry Wakefield."

"Larry is a bottom feeder. They don't really fight anyone, and their goal is to find good people in jams and then twist them," Chris said.

"Yeah, that whole blackmail thing wasn't right," Steven said, shaking his head.

"Did they tell you the details?" Chris asked.

Robin nodded. "Oh yes, we all had a group meeting and went over everything. It's important that we know how it happened so we can protect ourselves. It must have been awful for them to carry their caseloads, run their departments, and have that burden on deck."

"I'm sure the weight they felt was a lot like the hole going on onn the books," Chris said.

Robin waved the waiter down. "Young man, we will be eating with the Griggs." The waiter nodded and ran to the back.

Chris didn't even try to fight it anymore. His plan to have this conversation with Gina in any form of private venue was gone. As Robin talked about the meeting, he looked at her, and his chest tightened. What had happened to the woman who had fearlessly spoken about whatever she wanted. Where had his warrior woman gone? Not that she didn't do her part. She was implementing the project at a fast pace that was making everyone happy, but it wasn't what it used to be.

It wasn't going to happen tonight, but he had to talk to her to make things right again.

Twenty-four

Gina had decided that the awkward silence was enough. She thought Chris was going to bring it up during dinner but when Robin and Steven showed up, she gave up on that. No matter what, the issue had to be discussed. She had been mulling it over in her head about what Chris had said and she wasn't any closer to an answer.

Gina wasn't one to run from a problem so she called Chris over to meet her at the diner where Lucy worked. The diner had just opened, and she hoped Chris would get there before a crowd came. She thought neutral ground would be a better place to have this conversation.

Lucy slid into her booth.

"So, you're back," she said, raising her eyebrows.

Gina laughed at how open and carefree Lucy was.

"I'm back, what's up?'

"So, the hot guy you brought last time?"

"The one that is coming here today," Gina said with a smile.

"Mr. Right, or Mr. Right now? I mean, I'm not going to judge you because he looks hot enough to have either way."

Gina shook her head. "I'm not into Mr. Right now's."

"Well, if that's the case, let me know where you found him so I can see if there are any more."

"We work together, kind of. He started a new business venture and I'm helping him out."

Lucy sat back in the booth, nodding approvingly. "Good, he knows you come with skills and aren't looking for a handout."

Gina laughed. "I hadn't quite thought of it that way but it's true. I have a skill or two."

"Does he have any skills? You know you have to be careful, sometimes the ones that look the best, that *is* their skill," Lucy warned.

"No, he's got a skill or two as well, and money."

"Money? Well, that's a strike against him."

Gina was confused. "A strike against him?"

Lucy shrugged. "People with money are different."

"Really?"

"Let me tell you I make a respectable 17/hr. I met a guy. He made an easy 70k a year. He had all sorts of concerns I didn't. I liked him and I thought he would be good for me and one, but it was too much. Every time I turned around, there were some new rules. I couldn't go out the house at certain times because he was worried about me being robbed. When I told him I knew the people out in that spot, it only made it worse. So I'm telling you unless there is some serious compromising going on money can be a killer."

That was so true, thought Gina. In fact, wasn't that what she was working on now? Gina could feel the heat building behind her eyes. Could it really be this simple and this tragic? This decision wasn't just about what was good for her. This decision had to be about what would be best for Chris and Chymera too.

"Let me know when you're ready, my regulars are coming in. You okay?"

Gina looked up at Lucy and nodded. "Yes, I'm fine. Thank you."

"No problem."

Gina leaned back in the booth, closed her eyes, and took a deep breath. Now it was clear what had to be done. She just had to do it.

"You didn't order yet?"

She opened her eyes and there he was. He had such a strong jaw and a firm chin. How odd she never noticed before? He was truly an attractive man by parts and all together. Gina wasn't one to draw things out, and now that she knew what was needed, she wanted to rip the band-aid off the wound.

"I think the Center is running well. Everyone has a plan, and they're following it to the tee. The daily calls are helping to answer any questions. I've heard some people are going to you to get answers as well," she began.

Chris grinned. "It's been gratifying to be in on the ground floor and to be a part of something that gives me almost immediate satisfaction."

"I think that it's time for us to drop the engagement and for me to transition the last parts of the project to you."

She saw him fall back in the booth almost as if she had pushed him. His face went almost void of expression, and she could feel something in her shriveling.

"I was out of line when it came to Larry—"

"I shouldn't have confronted him for a lot of reasons, and yours were valid as well."

"It was efficient."

"Chris, I am efficient. I think of the shortest route to do things."

"There's nothing wrong with that. We can work on it."

"Work on this maybe and then what? I did a risk assessment, and the probability is high; this will happen again."

"Then we'll deal with it."

"I wanted to say thank you for letting me be a part of the Center. They are an amazing group of people that I'm better for having known."

"Gina we can—"

"I've already made plans to find an assignment."

Chris stopped and stared at her until she looked away. "Then there's nothing left to say?"

"No, there's nothing," she whispered.

He stood up and walked out the diner.

Gina blinked away the tears, and when she wasvsure he had gone, picked up a napkin and dabbed at the errant tears that refused to wait until she was home. She'd done the right thing and if she kept saying that to herself, maybe one day she'd believe it.

Over the next two days, she did everything by phone. She didn't dare go into the office because she hadn't gotten control of herself yet. Hour by hour, her emotions were all over the place. She had written lists of the pros and the cons of the relationship. She had done a Venn diagram on likes to see if any of what they did overlapped enough to compensate for his money.

She was at the point where ads that offered relationship help were starting to look good. She could work all day, but the hardest times were at night. At night she dreamed of him smiling, she remembered what it was like to be in his arms. More than anything else, she desperately wanted to know what it felt like to have that safe harbor again with another person.

She had done the right thing. She tried to drown her sorrows in food and chocolate but everything she touched somehow reminded her of him. She knew she would miss him, but this was more. It wasn't that a book was missing off the shelf. It wasn't like when she broke up with her previous boyfriend. The only thing she had missed with him was she had no one to go hiking with. Not having Chris around was like someone took a part of her, and now she was like a person who had lost a limb and was suffering from phantom pains in the missing limb.

If she were honest with herself, she knew the problem here was she wasn't just involved with the man. Chris had become her friend, her confidant and the one she could tell about her escapades. She'd trusted him, and when she thought about that loss, the tears came of their own accord.

Her head knew she had done the right thing. She just didn't know how long it would take to convince her heart that this was the best course of action.

Twenty-five

It had been a week since the diner. Chris sat at his desk in the Center looking at the walls covered with the mini whiteboards she used to create the project plans for the Center. He would open the notebook in front of him every so often as if he were going to write something, and then close it. When he looked at the computer screen, he could see the financials and the projections for the New Hope Center and it was all moving forward and coming into its own. He was looking at her legacy and her work.

He thought about Gina constantly. She laughed with him in his dreams and nothing else held his attention. He was going through the motions, but he wasn't enjoying anything. He had taken to keeping a square of chocolate in his desk, but he couldn't eat it without her.

The door burst open and he didn't even flinch. He knew eventually this would come. In came Robin, Steven, Michelle and Clara. They stood with their hands over their chests, looking at him in disapproval.

"I take it no one has come in here to say thank you for the growth we are experiencing," Chris muttered.

He opened the drawer and saw the chocolate, but still, he couldn't eat it.

"Something has been going on at the Center and we felt it would be fair and appropriate to come to you as we are the management team," Robin said.

"Go for it," Chris prompted.

"Gina." Clara came forward and straightened her back and then looked over her shoulder at Michelle who nodded her on. "She hasn't been around, and we know that there was something fishy about your engagement and she hasn't shown up in the office in a week."

"Yes?"

"So, we want to make sure you understand our position when it comes to Gina," Robin said.

"If you are here to tell me how to handle Gina, you're too late," he growled.

Robin said sternly. "This is about Gina. We all love her, and she's done so much for us."

"She spoke to me when I thought it was over," Michelle said.

"It's funny to see you all here now. Did any of you tell her how valued she was when she was here?" he growled.

Steven looked confused. "We've all visited her in her office at one time or another. She's given us all suggestions for work and life. She's a good person and we want to look out for her."

"Well, while this meeting is sweet, it's unnecessary. Gina and I are no longer an item."

Michelle leaned over to Clara. "I told you all he was going to mess it up. He wasn't the right kind of guy."

"Was it so obvious?" Chris asked. The problem was, Michelle was right. He had gone and messed it up.

"Perhaps this was all for the best, unless you really are interested in her?" Robin prompted.

"I want to marry her," Chris said quietly.

"Whew! I'm so glad because I just couldn't think how I was going to get the jump on you to make Gina a respectable woman," Steven said.

"Well, like I said, you're all too late. She broke it off with me," Chris confessed.

"That can't be, she loves you," Robin said. "If you had seen her when she talked about you, you would have known right away."

"Unless he messed it up," murmured Michelle.

"Go to her and ask her to marry you and tell her you love her," Steven said. Everyone in the room nodded in agreement.

"I don't think that is going to work," Chris said. "As much as it pains me to say it, Michelle is right. I have two things going against me. The first one is I was scared for her life and I told her she was endangering herself and others by confronting Larry on her own. The other is, I can't do a project plan," he explained.

After he had said the first reason, they had all started to talk about ways to fix that. When he said the second one the room went silent.

"I'm not sure I understand what you're saying," Michelle asked. "We're talking about the relationship?"

Letting out a huge sigh Chris explained. "Gina explained that her dream man will be able to do project plans like her. She thinks a project-plan mind will give her a stable life,"

"It seems kind of weird you wouldn't know how to do a project plan and you run Chymera," Steven said.

"Well, let me tell you my project plans have about four steps: I determine the scope, I determine how much money I want to spend. I assign people tasks, I look at end result."

Everyone in the room nodded, giving him encouragement.

"Everyone look on the walls, that is a project plan. Gina thinks her dream man should be able to do that." Chris said.

"I have to say, she has more than four steps," Clara said.

"Well, it can't be that hard. You run Chymera. Learn how to do it and then ask her," Robin said.

Chris laughed. "Have you looked at those? Not just anyone could do that."

"I'll get someone who can teach you," Michelle volunteered. "That is if you want to try, but she's not cheap."

Chris smiled at Michelle. "I think I can afford it."

The day was getting away from him. It started this morning with the group wanting to know about Gina and then finding a way to get her back. Now his sister was here this afternoon and once again he had to wonder how the day was going to end.

"You've been walking around like you just lost your best friend and your dog. Would you like to tell me what is going on?" His sister she strode into his office.

"It's a bit early for me to say how it's all going to work out so—"

"So, now you're going to be vague with me?"

"If all of the stars align, I'm working on getting Gina to say yes to marrying me," Chris confessed.

"Is your current depressed state of mind related to the goal, and is this really a question? What woman would say no to you?"

"It's complicated Julia. I haven't asked her, but I don't think she'll say yes as she was the one who decided to end our relationship."

"Well, it seems like you have work to be done."

"I may not be up to the task."

Julia frowned at him. "Chris, of course you are up to the task."

"Really, as much as I appreciate your words of wisdom, the fact of the matter is that Gina may say no to me."

"Then I suggest you put on your thinking cap and find a way. But be careful of Gina's feelings."

"So, I know why the rest of them would like me to be with Gina. I'm a little lost on your rationale, sister."

"Chris, the world is always black and white for you. Family is what matters here. I had my own issues with the Center. I saw you working on it, and I couldn't bring myself to help you. You have no idea how much you look like father. It made me realize I still have some issues to address with my past." Julia closed her eyes and let out a large sigh.

Chris wanted to go to Julia, but he needed to clear this once and for all.

"Why, Julia? Gina told me about how you spoke to her. The things you said to her about her place in the business. Why would you say that?"

Julia took a deep breath and looked him in the eye. "I said that because you look so much like our father. I said it because one day we were talking about what should be done if we can't fix the Center and the next, you had a woman who had come over and you no longer wanted to give up the Center. You were talking about this new purpose you had. It was becoming you and her, there was no place for me in it.

"Dad made rash decisions and didn't tell anyone in the early days. You weren't exposed to the uncertainty that me and mom went through. When he was with you, it was always a steady picture but there were nights he would argue with mom over an idea someone else had told him. I couldn't see beyond those memories when I saw this place and how it appeared you were acting…"

"Julia—"

Julia cut him off and turned, looking around the office.

"I have to take my part of this as well. I let Larry go. I did it in public, and it was necessary, but I should have managed it better. I thought you being here at the Center would get old and you would leave, but you were much more tenacious than I gave you credit for.

Now, here we are. These last couple of days you have looked pretty down little brother, and I love you. If there is something I can do to help then let me know."

Chris got up and went to Julia.

"Since we're having a confession moment. I must tell you that I was always in awe of Dad because he kicked his habit and found a way to bring himself back so he could run the company. He didn't try to sugar coat it. He had a problem, he worked on it and then he went on.

"While I admired his spirit, it was you who I looked up to. You always did what was best for Chymera. You went along with whatever I came up with, and when a couple of my deals—which you had told me not to do— went south, you never said I told you so. So, you are right Julia. I am like Dad, but I've been polished by you and it helped me be the person I am today. I wouldn't cut you out, you're family and if all works out, I'll be counting on you to welcome Gina."

Twenty-six

The next day Chris was standing in front of a desk looking at the blank whiteboards. The boards had been cleaned several times and still, he didn't have anything to show for the hours of work he had done.

"Let's try again, Griggs," Cora Thalmine said as she sat in her chair dressed in a light green linen dress.

"The key to a project plan is understanding the steps. Every project begins with initiation, planning, execution, monitoring, and control and closure."

"That seems like a lot of steps to say, 'Let's go right.' All of this documentation and I won't have any time to do any real work. I need four boxes and that has served me well enough."

Cora smiled indulgently. "I can see how you might believe that has been working but it only works because you are leading the project and not sharing the responsibility of a project. So, let's go over this again so we can develop a plan that others will be able to assist in. Remember, project management is not just about getting to the end goal it is also about communicating to others and working as a team."

Chris turned to Cora and she handed him the papers to start with. Cora waited until he had taken the paper from her hands. "Griggs, try to act as if you are not the CEO of a company and that you may have to work with others."

"Well, I am the CEO and they do have to listen to me and maybe they should because I only need four boxes for my thoughts while the rest of them need all this to communicate basic ideas."

Cora's smile tightened. "Let's take your thoughts and put them on the boards. When we see items as bullet points then we can make sure we are all on the same page about where we should be going and what we should be doing. We want to move together as a unit."

"We would be a unit if everyone followed me. Besides what is the point of the plan and buy-in if I am going to have to fix it no matter what?"

Cora smiled sweetly. "Then maybe you should decide if you want to run a company where we share ideas or your own mini country where you are a dictator and the only opinion that matters is your opinion?"

Chris went to the boards and started writing out the plan. "Chymera is built on being open, so no, I don't want to foster a dictatorship."

Cora smiled. "I think the problem is you are trying to do it all at once. Go one step at a time. If you take your time to itemize it all you'll find that it will go smoother. Remember, all the steps are equally important. If you do that then everyone will not only understand what you want, they will be able to give feedback on the feasibility of the idea."

"Fine, I'll start with step one again." Chris went to a blank board and started writing. By the time he was on the fifth sentence, Cora cleared her throat. Chris looked over his shoulder. "You really want me to use the bullet points, don't you?"

"Yes, if you do, you'll find that it makes your thoughts concise," Cora said slightly amused.

"I'm thinking you are having so much fun at this you would have done this for free."

"I have to admit, this is way more entertaining than I thought it would be. Considering the person you are doing it for, I'm touched by your effort and amused looking at you trying to document what you do automatically."

"I don't do this," Chris replied.

"You do Griggs. The issue is you do it in your head and quickly. The problem you're having is sharing that information with anyone else at a regular pace. I know you know how to do this, you are just used to giving it to people when they need it instead of writing the whole process out."

"So, you're saying my problem is?"

"Patience, Griggs. Talent you have. It's patience that's beating you. But have no fear, I have patience enough for us both."

"Great, why can't I just buy that?"

Cora laughed. "Enough talking back to the board. Step by step."

He went back to the board and began to write out the steps in his head. He couldn't believe he was doing this. It was so crazy to think people lived like this. Just when he thought he would give up he thought of Gina. He hoped she would give him credit for trying. She was so giving to everyone else he was counting on her good nature to help him out as well.

Would he be able to provide a plan to her, he wasn't sure but he would still give it a shot. He would do all that he could to make this better.

Someone was knocking on her door. Cora had called her several times today. She knew eventually she'd show up, but Gina was hoping she had some more time.

"Gina, it's me."

It was him.

Chris.

She wanted to see him so bad. Was he well? Was everyone okay at the Center? Before she even realized it, she was the door. Once again, her head was being pushed to the side and her heart had her hand on the doorknob. When the door opened, she froze.

He had a five o'clock shadow, his hair had that finger-combed look—he looked good. She couldn't speak, she just stared at him. If she spoke, she'd have to tell him to go away and right now she didn't think she could do it.

"I want you to know that I need you and we need each other. I don't have a real seven-step plan but I can't even make the plan without you. Will you let me in?" he asked.

"We spoke before and—"

"Gina, I need you to be my safe harbor, don't turn me away."

She blinked and then stepped aside so he could enter. "Chris—"

"Hold on." She watched him pull out a rolled-up piece of paper and then go to her kitchen table and spread it out. "Okay, this is the rough plan. I think we can fill it in with some other items, but we can discuss it as we go."

Gina looked over his shoulder and saw the seven steps of a plan and then saw Chris' notes, 'Ask Gina'. She touched each one and knew this was going to work.

"Now, listen. I was wrong about Larry, we can fix that. The plan thing I'm going to have to pick up later. I know you said you needed a planner, and I can do this. It's going to take me a little longer, but is that going to stop you from doing the right thing for us both?"

Gina blinked the tears that threatened to fall. She couldn't believe he had tried to do this. It wasn't the most elegant proposal, but it was a very Griggs proposal. "What right thing are you talking about?"

"Don't be coy. You're supposed to be transparent in the plan. Do you see it in your plan to marry me? Because it's in mine and we should sync up."

Gina stood up and folded her arms over her chest. "That's my proposal? Where are the flowers and the chocolate?"

"Write it in the plan and I'll make sure it goes through the proper channels and gets approved," he said with a smile.

"An approval process huh?" Gina said.

Chris pulled her into his arms. "Oh yes, the process is very important in planning."

"This plan is looking like it was just thrown together with little to no effort," she sniffed.

"No effort? If you had been there when Cora was laughing at me and—"

"You asked Cora for help?"

"Yes, I had to and she kept erasing my notes and—"

"I'll marry you."

"What?"

"You heard me. I'll marry you."

He pulled her in his arms and swung her around the kitchen. "I'm going to send Cora the biggest gift!" He placed her back on her feet and leaned down to kiss her. He kissed her while they both laughed at his reaction.

"I'll make this work Gina, I promise."

"I know Chris."

"I spoke with Julia, she's onboard too."

"That's good Chris."

"Making you happy will be my number one goal."

She pulled his head down and gave him a kiss on his lips and then one on his chin. She looked into his eyes and savored the feeling of being in his arms.

"I missed you,"

"Nevermore Gina."

"In case you don't know. I love you."

Chris dropped his forehead to hers. "I'm glad because I've loved you since the first project we did in school."

"And you let me go?"

He pulled her into his embrace. "You see it was all part of the plan that—"

They both fell out laughing. Gina pulled on his collar and kissed him again and then cleared her throat.

Chris smiled. "Yeah, it's a challenge but I love you too, Gina."

"Eh, you'll have to work on your delivery," she said before he pulled her back into his embrace and kissed her again.

Epilogue

Michael Thalman wasn't big on parties. People who sought him out needed something or wanted him to do something for him. The only reason he was here in the back booth of a diner he'd never heard of was because of a woman he could never forget, his ex-wife Cora Thalman.

He had arrived half an hour earlier to the diner. Cora was sitting with a friend and employee, Gina Kenyon. Sitting across from Michael was Christopher Griggs, Gina's fiance if the rings were to be believed. In about an hour, the diner would be hosting a small party for the employees of New Hope Medical Center. It was Christopher Grigg's new project. With the success of his new project, Christopher had opted not to go to the children's retreat. The children's retreat gathered businessmen from different industries and put them on a camp to give back to underprivileged kids.

Since Christopher wasn't going Michael had asked him to give his spot to Cora. Cora had said yes.

Michael loved Cora. Cora was still that vivacious woman he had med ten years ago. Her hair was a honey brown that beckoned him to touch it. During their marriage, he'd always loved touching her hair as she lay on his chest. Michael remembered when she would sleep in his arms and he'd listen to her light snoring that she always denied in the morning.

She was the woman he had dreamed of but certainly hadn't been worthy. Cora had embraced him with all her love and made him into a better man. Then they had lost a child and the glow that was Cora had dimmed. One day they had been living the dream and three weeks later, he'd been served divorce papers.

Michael had seen an opportunity, and he was going to take it. He needed to find out if he could get Cora to remember who they had been and what they could do together because living without Cora was much living at all.

His friend Chris cleared his throat.

Michael held up his hand. "You've already said it's a bad idea."

"It is, but if this is what you want to do, I understand."

"Do you?"

"Now that I have Gina in my life, I understand that a man would push the limits to get a second chance at paradise."

Michael looked at his friend. "I guess you do get it. So what did you want to say?"

"Did you consider that showing up like this may do more harm to you both?"

Michael leaned over to see Cora smiling but her eyes weren't lit up with joy. He heard her laughing but it wasn't the hearty laugh that you could tell came from her bell. Michael shook his head and looked at Chris.

"I've got to try this because right now, neither one of us is really living at all without the other."

I hope you enjoyed Gina and Chris's story. If you'd like to read more about the women in Vision Consulting and the men who are looking for a second chance with them. Check out *Remember Us* for book three of the Love Endures series and read Cora's story.

Sign up to my newsletter to receive updates on new releases, sale promotions, and free books.

susanwarnerauthor.com

www.ingramcontent.com/pod-product-compliance
Lightning Source LLC
Chambersburg PA
CBHW071820190726
48292CB00005B/1530